Angelic Confessions: Special Edition

Jan Marie

Published by Jan Marie, 2023.

ANGELIC CONFESSIONS: SPECIAL EDITION

First edition. September 15, 2023.

Copyright © 2023 Jan Marie.

ISBN: 979-8223946373

Written by Jan Marie.

Table of Contents

Dedication

Angelic Confessions: Special Edition has been a long time coming. While I released it originally in 2013, like any creator, there were things I wanted to do better.

To my mother, who encouraged me.

To my husband for never letting me stop.

To my three boys, Zachery, Aidan, and Zane, for letting mommy write.

So now read Angelic Confessions like you have never read it before.

-Jan Marie

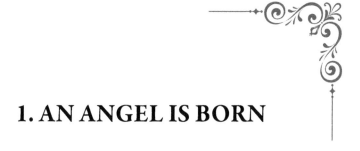

1. AN ANGEL IS BORN

Where's Brother? My brother? Our warm cocoon no longer housed my constant companion. Suddenly, I was gone, feeling embraced in familiar warmth. I knew this warmth; it was Mother. I knew I loved my mother very much, but I didn't know why. Yet, why did not matter; I just did. What I mostly recall about her was her flame-red curls. You see, my brother and I were rare miracles. We had heard the

talks from voices on the outside as we grew inside our mother. They would come and talk to us often while she slept. They would whisper that we were a special breed, that we would be superior. My brother eagerly reveled in this idea, but I did not understand what was so wonderful about us being superior. How did they know?

Brother often scowled at me for my lack of interest. I did not care as my interest was for our mother. She was always so sad. I had often wondered if she was not happy that we were growing inside her? It didn't matter, I was out now. I began to cry in my Mother's arms still wondering where brother was.

"Do not worry my child," she whispered as she started to rock me. She started to hum a sweet song that lulled me to sleep as I dreamed of a wonderful place. A garden of lush green and waterfalls.

WE GREW RAPIDLY, MY brother was already reaching full-grown adult form, but I did not. Due to this we were kept further apart, living

1

in separate tents in the encampment we lived in. At night, though, brother would often sneak over to see me while Mother slept.

"Why are you not reaching your full form?" He asked me one night.

"I like being a child. It's fun."

"So is being in full form," he smiled. "The things we can do..." he reached over brushing a strand of hair from my face. For some strange reason, a part of my heart ached for that. I loved my brother very much and missed him, but it wasn't right.

"All I've seen you do is discuss strategy with the Elders. Sounds boring, " I scoffed turning back to my toys.

"You belong to me, little sister!" he scolded me as he rose to his feet.

"You will CHANGE!" I felt the prick of tears welling in my eyes as I watched him walk away. Darkness; that is what was in him, and I was drawn to that same darkness too. Did my brother hate me now? If I did this...change, would I be allowed to see him more? No more of these secret visits.

UPON SEEING MY BROTHER again, the next morning outside the tent while me and mother were washing food by the river, I realized I was wrong about thinking my brother hated me.

"Acim!" I said, my face lit up at the sight of him. He smiled in return as he knelt down holding out his arms for me to come to him. I started for him when Mother grabbed me, crushing me to her. "You will not touch her!"

"Well, I still have Mommy to play with then don't I?" My brother slyly grinned then rose turning on his heels as he walked away.

Mother buried her face in my long dark locks, crying. I did not understand all this.

All I knew was that his words had made Mother cry. I reached my hand up to sooth Mother, touching her cheek. I froze as the world around me went black. The horrifying truth swirled into my mind of what my brother and I were meant to

be: we were meant to be killers. We were meant to be breeders, to create an army of our unique kind. We were a new race that would overtake the children of Heaven. They tried others, but they were all a waste. My hand slipped from, my mother's face as I cried too.

I NEXT REMEMBER AWAKING to heavy panting as I heard a familiar heartbeat pumping fast against me.

"Mother?" I said as I realized we were running, just her and I. "Where is brother?"

"Shh, child, please. He is lost to us."

Brother is lost? I felt her fear rise as we suddenly stopped. She rested against a tree still clutching me tightly to her as I heard her life-beat start to grow slower. I started to fall back to sleep to its soothing, declining sound. I thought it was horrid

of me, to be soothed by her life decreasing.

"Please, Mother, don't die." I whispered sleepily. I could not keep my eyes open as I drifted off into slumber again.

"Do you think she's alright? All she's done is sleep."

VOICES? WHEN I OPENED my eyes slightly, I saw two large shadow figures hovering above me.

"Yes, see she is fine; now bring her to our Lord." I closed my eyes again not caring what they said.

"Aye...open your eyes. Open your eyes now, little one. I know you can hear me."

Voices again! Ugh! Could I ever sleep?

"Sleep time is over; it is time to wake up." A deep booming voice bellowed. I opened my eyes to see a face illuminated in a bright white glow looking down at me. It was a man and a warm, soft smile crossed his features, then the bright white light returned again as his voice spoke.

"Hello. I am your father."

"Father? I said wincing away a bit at the brightness that was him. "What about my brother? Do you know where he is?" I asked curiously.

"I am sorry I do not." The man's face returned and I could see his features soften as if it felt my concern, "But you are my daughter, and I love you very much."

Something inside me instantly wanted to be his daughter, so I accepted it. He was my Father, nothing more, nothing less. Forgotten was everything about my brother, my mother, and the dark destiny that had awaited me.

EVEN SO, SOME THINGS could not be stopped since I continued to grow. A growing, young "angel" was quite different for Father, I am sure. I thought I had stopped it. I wanted to be a child forever! As an aid to help me comprehend, he showed me the humans he had created, describing how I experienced the same growth as them only, perhaps, it seemed quicker. Oh, that didn't matter anymore as I instantly fell in love with the humans. I insisted I wanted to live like them. I wanted the prettiest young lady dresses and most beautiful trinkets just like theirs. Father enthusiastically obliged assigning me my own chambers and showering me with the prettiest dresses and trinkets sometimes straight from earth itself. The only human concept I did not like was the concept of a "bed." I much preferred sleeping cuddled next to Father's feet while he worked, or better yet snuggle in his arms. I would often sneak out of my chambers when Father tucked me into bed to find him.

"Aye," he would say in his booming voice accentuating on the "A" as he sensed my presence before I even stepped into the room. He would turn around seeing me as I looked up at him, giving my best adorable pout. Father would sigh as he scooped me up, squeezing me in his warmth.

"Why are you so hard to resist, little one." He would smile then snuggle me more. I would just giggle and latch onto him tighter, falling into his enormous love. I did not know the why either, all I knew was I all had to do was look adoringly up at Father to melt his heart to my way. It was the innocent seduction of a child.

SOON MY STUDIES WERE to begin. I was to learn the history and etiquette of how to be a proper angel. I obeyed Father completely and without thought: he was my father. After the completion of my lessons, Father continued to humor my fascination with

humans, allowing me to peer down on them. I, in particular, enjoyed watching children my age.

"Can I play with them, Father?" I asked one day.

"I am sorry, Aye, you can not. You must stay here at home with me."

My heart saddened as disappointment started to rise up in my chest, the sting of tears welling in my eyes. It felt like a dam was about to burst inside me.

"Would you like to go into the gardens and see the animals next?" Father chimed in.

"Animals?" I asked looking up at him with interest, wiping my budding tears away. Father smiled, relieved he had managed to stop an onslaught of tears as he took my hand. I knew that Father's only wish was for me was to be happy, and I was. But I heard the hushed tones and whispers others spoke of me when I walked down the marbled halls with Father. I heard their whispered words.

"There she is...!"

"Oh, but did you hear..."

"...She has our Lord under her spell."

"I heard she could kill us all..."

I'd close my eyes tight trying to block out the whispers with all my might. Did they now I could hear them?! What, did all that mean? I knew Father said I was to never leave the tower that was our home. I never really interacted with anyone else aside from Father and the strange angel with the flame-curls. Then there were the dreams. Did the others see my dreams? Nightmares were more like it. In the dreams, It's always the same. Me standing alone on a battlefield of broken wings and blood. I knew I was the cause of this destruction,

and I reveled in it.

ONE DAY, FATHER CUT our lessons short so that he might introduce me to his assistants. As a result, he made sure I was dressed most presentable. I wore a mid-length white dress that flourished out, thanks to the tons of petticoats underneath. The waist was accentuated with a thick a pink ribbon sash that met in a pretty bow in the back. I was always put in a dress that had some sort of pink or red color in it. This was to show without uttering a word, who I was and to whom I belonged to. Red was the color representation of my mother, who sat on the high council with Father. To touch me, even acknowledge me was forbidden unless stated otherwise. Today, thought I was going to meet some new angels. I walked down the grand marbled halls with Father to our destination. We passed the large, arched windows as the outside blue skies beckoned to me to fly. I always wondered what lurked outside these walls I was tied to. I was either near Father's side or I was given to the angel with long, red curls who did not tell me her name.

Her constant presence was perplexing to me. Father said she liked me, that I am special. It had been a long while since a young angel like me roamed the tower halls. I wasn't buying it, but accepted it. If Father said I was to spend time with her, I obeyed, though a bit begrudgingly. Not that she was horrible. She was often kind, letting me comb her long red curls and adorn them with the white wild flowers that grew in the gardens. I came out of my thoughts as we approached a row of male angels dressed in regal attire lined up to greet us. They all bowed in unison as Father approached. It was then, that one stepped forward and knelt on one knee before me. He smiled. He had long hair like ebony silk that was tied in a queue while his eyes were a pale autumn brown...almost amber. This was Uriel.

"Hello, it's a pleasure to have a young one running around the tower again," he spoke.

"There will be no running," Father boomed, correcting him. Uriel looked up at Father, then down clearing his throat as he rose taking his place back among the Others. Raphael was next and it was he who was to teach me now. I was to

become a healer like him. Raphael knelt down on one knee before me with a smile that reached his aquamarine eyes, glistening brightly against his fair skin and pale blonde hair.

"Hello, Princess. Are you not sweetly beautiful? Father's definitely going to have to keep an eye on you," he winked. Uriel elbowed Raphael in the head. "Ow!

What?" Raphael said, looking up at Uriel. I giggled at their banter. Finally, there was Michael, stoic in stature, his long wavy dark brown hair was untethered from any bonds. He bowed formally to me, then looked up at me taking my hand. "It is a pleasure, little miss." he smiled. "We'll have fun don't worry." he Winked. I smile, feeling heat rise to my cheeks. Father then breaks the entrancement, saying there was also Gabriel who was away at the time but I would meet him soon. I curtseyed to all saying it was nice to meet them.

AS FATHER AND I DEPARTED from them, we continued on with our day. Father took me to one of the many lush green gardens in the tower. When we entered, I saw Uriel standing with another angel under a large oak tree that stood in the center of the gardens. They both looked like tall night and day statues, Uriel with his silken black hair and the other with flowing white hair. They caught sight of us and bowed to their Lord as we approached. I caught sight of the white-haired angel glance at me as he then disgustedly looked away. This was Gabriel, and I concluded quickly in my mind that he did not like me. It seemed I was either adored or despised around here. Father stroked my hair making me come out of my doom and gloom thoughts as he said he needed to talk to Gabriel about some business, and that Uriel would watch over me until he returned. I nodded as I watched both of them go.

"Come, little one, would you like to hear a story?" Uriel asked. I looked up at him as tears started to brew in my eyes. He came closer to embrace me.

"My, my, what is wrong?"

"Father..." I whimpered.

"Your Father is an important man and sometimes he cannot take you with him.

My, has our Lord spoiled you." I pulled away, wiping my tears with the back of my hand. "So, would you like to hear a story," Uriel asked again with a smile. I nodded as he took my hand. We found a lovely spot under the large oak to sit. "You know about the humans, right?" he inquired as though he were testing me.

"Yes, Father showed them to me."

"They are quite fascinating, hmm?"

I looked down coyly, playing with the hem of my dress. "A bit..." I said, feeling Uriel brush my hair back from my neck. I then feel his breath hit my neck in a whisper and I freeze. Suddenly, jerking flashes of screams and clashing swords played out before me in blood-curdling images of fights and slaughter of angels.

"Aye!" I blinked, coming out of my vision, surprised to see that Father had returned for me.

"Father!" I beamed as if nothing happened rising up to embrace him.

"Oh, you missed me so much; was Uriel that bad?"

"No," I said looking up at Father's adoring face. I turned to Uriel. "Thank you, Uriel; I enjoyed my time with you."

"It's been my pleasure, dear," he said as he rose to his feet. He nodded his head to Father. "It is done, my Lord," he said quietly. Father reached out to Uriel, gripping him on the shoulder.

"Thank you, Uriel."

What I did not know, was the magic spells and binding Father used to seal my memories...my darkness always had the risk of coming undone. I was meant to kill. Even though I showed no dark interest like my brother, it was better to be safe than sorry, and Father knew his brother would not play fair to win me back.

"Care to accompany me on the rest of my daily duties, my lady?" Father asked. I curtsied formally to him. "It would be my pleasure, my Lord." Father chuckled. "Very nice." I looked up at him and smiled proudly. That was all I wanted, was for Father to be proud of me. His approval was everything to me. I accompanied Father on his duties once again as we walked the halls. He paused as we reached some stairs leading down. I froze, knowing I was to never leave the upper levels of the tower. Father must have sensed my nervousness and I heard him chuckle. "It is okay," he said, giving my hand a squeeze. "As long as I am with you, this is okay."

I looked up at Father, unsure, but he just smiled as he gave my hand another squeeze and we headed down. After pressing on, we reached the bottom level of the tower and continued to walk down the grey stone corridor. The lower levels of the tower weren't as greatly crafted as the upper levels which were of a grand marble and gold. The end of the hall opened up onto the training ground of the guards which spilled out into a round forested arena. This was where Father's soldiers trained. I watched these angels as they sparred, their swords clanking. The sound of metal against metal, until something caught my eye. I saw three male angels striding towards us. They were known as Father's Elite Guards, dressed quite differently from the traditional angelic robes most wore. Instead, they wore black leggings with shiny black boots, and a double-breasted tunic with high collars trimmed in gold that matched with their gold belts that cinched at their waists. Each had their hair length groomed short, too, which was unique as well for an angel, but quite handsome on them. They stopped in front of us and the two guards on the ends, one with blonde hair, and the other with copper brown curls, knelt down before Father leaving the dark-haired guard still standing and he then bows. I attached myself to father's side, hiding behind his robes as the dark-haired one looked up and spoke.

"Your orders have been fulfilled, my Lord."

"Thank you, Pio. We can discuss this further when a certain young lady is not present." I looked up at Father, concerned. Was I in his way? He just smiled down at me as he stroked my hair to soothe me, letting me know everything was alright.

"This is my newest, by the way."

"A little attached, my Lord," the blonde said, glancing up with a slight smirk.

"Yes, indeed, and I to her," Father chuckled. I saw the dark-haired one, called

Pio, step over as he knelt down to me.

"I'm Pio, nice to meet you." He smiled offering his hand. I looked at him, wide-eyed that he actually spoke to me sincerely. I heard Father clear his throat as I let go of his side and did the proper, ladylike thing.

"Nice to meet you as well." I said, curtseying before him.

"Such a proper princess." he smiled.

"I am NOT!" I scoffed and kicked his shin. I cringed as I felt Father's hands come crashing down on my shoulders tightly. Crap! I was in for it now.

"It's okay." Pio said, rubbing his shin with a slight grimace on his face.

"Yeah, Pio has that effect on females." grinned the copper-haired one.

"Shut up!" Pio glared back at him. I threw myself into his arms, wrapping my own around his neck. I felt him stiffen a bit; I knew I had surprised him. In fact, I had surprised myself with my bold action.

"I'm sorry!" I cried as I buried my face in his neck to stop the tears, I felt brewing. He unwrapped my arms from around him, but did not let go of my hands as he held them to his chest.

"It's okay, my lady," he smiled gently, kissing my hands. "You'll be hard to forget." he winked and smiled. I felt Father's hands on my shoulders again, softer this time.

"We should take our leave now, thank you all." he said as he nodded to them. We left, returning to the upper levels.

PIO

I watched them go. "My Gods the child was beautiful." I thought. I knew, now, why Father seemed to covet her so. You just wanted to protect her sweet innocence forever. It seemed nothing was innocent anymore on earth or in heaven. It did not matter though; I had to brush the sweet girl out of my mind. That evening I went to visit Father to give him my full report. The guard outside Father's chambers stood at attention upon seeing me.

"Our Lord is expecting you." He bowed, opening the door. I walked inside and saw Father at his desk.

"Pio, my son," Father said as he rose. "I have a new assignment for you. And you only." He urged.

"My Lord? Care to elaborate?" I asked suspiciously. Father chuckled.

"Never one to beat around the bush I see...well there are some concerns with the humans. I am assembling a group to be 'Watchers.'"

"Watchers? But my-"

"Your men will be reassigned."

"Thank you, Father, I am honored." I bowed as I agreed to become a part of this new team of Watchers. The problem was, I never got to be. I was to watch over something far more precious than just humans.

AYE

I knew Father had to be upset with me. I don't know what came over me! I tried to act like nothing happened as we reached the upper levels.

"Um... he was nice, Father."

"Then why did you kick him, my daughter?"

I winced. Yep, he was not happy. I stopped bowing my head.

"I don't know...I... sometimes...well Raphael called me Princess-"

"You need to control these outbursts of yours. A daughter of mine will not act out in such violence!"

"*Kill him*!" A voice stabbed my head. I gasped falling to my knees. "*Kill the children of heaven!*"

"AYE!" Father's voice shook me. I blinked, finding myself on the floor with Father gripping me tightly.

"Did I do something wrong, Father?" I asked, wondering why Father had me in such a tight grip. Why did he look so worried? He pulled me to him.

"Nothing. I just love you, my daughter. My sweet child." I embraced Father back, hoping to dissuade the concern in his heart. I knew something had happened, but my mind would not let me remember it. I somehow knew, though, my nightmares were creeping into my daylight.

2. HEALING WAYS

On the next day, Father took me to Raphael's chambers to begin my lessons to
become a healer. Father knocked on Raphael's door, which opened immediately to reveal the angel, all smiles and dressed in his creamed colored angelic robes. His blonde hair was tied loosely behind his back as he stepped to the side, bowing extravagantly.

"Welcome, my Lord and Lady. Come in."

"Please, go sit on the chaise, dear; Raphael will be with you shortly."

Father motioned to the white and gold cushioned chaise against the far wall inside the room. I obeyed and walked over to it, taking a seat before looking over at the door. Father and Raphael were speaking quietly, so I let my eyes wander about the room. It had a warmth to it, with its walls a dark forest green. A tall, dark wooden shelf stood against the far wall in front of me, lined with jars filled with healing herbs of some kind. To my left, sat a desk facing a wall made of entire glass, which showed the green of plants and colorful flowers inside that assumed was a greenhouse where Raphael grew all his healing herbs. I sensed Father, and I looked back over to him. He smiled at me, then nodded, taking his leave. I was a little saddened, but my curiosity as to what Raphael had to teach me won out my emotions to lash out in a fit of tears.

"Let's see now, shall we," Raphael said as he closed the door, sealing us inside. He walked into the next room only to re-emerge quickly, holding a small potted plant in his hands that was wilted. I tilted my head as I felt the plant's pain.

"It's hurting, Raphael," I said as I furrowed my brow, not taking my eyes off the poor plant. He knelt down in front of me.

"Yes, you are right, and with our gifts, we can make it better." He hovered his hand over the plant and a golden glow formed under his palm, engulfing it in a golden light. Then, the glow then dissipated, revealing the plant back to its bright green, leafy beauty.

"I can do this?" I whispered questioningly as I looked up to Raphael.

"Yes, it is in you; we just need to switch it around."

"Switch" I asked, puzzled.

"Shh," he said as he put a finger to his lips and set the plant aside on the floor. He then laid his hands on my shoulders and closed his eyes. I wondered what was going on when he opened them again to poke me on the forehead.

"Boo!"

I gasped, falling back against the chaise; I did not know I was literally on the edge of my seat.

"See!" Raphael smiled, rising to his feet. "We just needed to refocus your energies." Refocus energies my foot I thought as I scowled at him. What I didn't know was at that moment, I had officially transcended into a healer. It made perfect sense as I was initially meant to kill. Why not reprogram me toward the total opposite, healing. For you see, a healer's oath was that no blood shall ever stain a healer's hands. It was a perfect fail-safe. Raphael went back into the room and returned with another sick plant.

"Now you try," he said, holding it out to me. I paused a bit, then relaxed, closing my eyes, reaching my senses out, connecting with the plant. I felt its pain, its thirst. I then quelled it with a golden light, opening my eyes to see that the golden glow had physically manifested around the plant and then faded. I smiled as the withering plant before me was green and bursting with tiny white flowers once again. I looked to Raphael, who smiled back at me.

"Can I have it? I will take care of it." He paused a bit, looking, uncertainly, at me before smiling again. "You may," he said. I smiled, hugging the plant close to me. Raphael chuckled as he rose to his feet again. I knew I had pleased him very much, in just my first lesson. After that, I had lessons with Raphael every day while my evenings were spent with Father, where we'd dined together and I showed him what I had learned that day. Father was proud of my growing abilities, which made me even happier.

I KEPT GROWING, AND at the age of twelve, Father introduced me to music. I took a liking to the piano, bonding with it instantly. Father informed me that all angels had musical talent and that the piano was now mine. I should have been content, but I kept longing for the humans more and more. I hadn't looked at them in such a long time. What is my fascination with them? Maybe it was the freedom that they had. Father would say I had freedom, but it was only the freedom to remain in the tower. "It is for your protection Aye. I love you, my child." Father would say. But I was starting to resent his love, which I thought was awful of me. Those soul-stirring voices that still haunted me were right. Blood be my destiny. I had become a healer now, but it did not quell the dark, seductive voices that would still often whisper in my ear as I slept. I sat alone on the edge of my bed with these thoughts rolling in my mind. I toyed with a beautiful music box Father had given me. Why could I not be free like the humans? Frustration rose in me as I gripped the music box and flung it across the room, hitting my mirror, and sending a large crack down its middle as it thudded to the ground.

"Aye?" I blinked, seeing the sight of a distorted Michael through the large crack in the mirror. When did he arrive? I spun around as he entered, closing the door behind him.

"I will have the mirror repaired for you. No one will know." He said, crossing over to me. I could not take his kindness as I broke into blinding tears, feeling Michael wrap his arms around me. "I know, little miss." I heard him comfort me as he stroked my hair, brushing it away from my neck.

"You are Heaven's best-kept secret, aren't you?"

"Secret?" I said, frowning, pulling away. He just smiled, caressing a lingering tear away.

"Oh, it's not time for us to play yet, little miss. Forget our little conversation." He said, stroking his finger on my lips. Then, blackness.

THE NEXT DAY, FATHER left me once again in Raphael's care for my lesson. As I walked down the marbled halls with the great healer, he talked about something I wasn't really paying attention to. I swore he talked just because he liked hearing the sound of his voice. I stopped, unable to take any more of his talking. I watched Raphael continue to walk, chatting away without me. He did not even notice I was gone! I grinned, slyly, taking a step back, then another. He had to catch now, but he didn't, still carrying on. I gathered my dress and dashed back down the hall towards the Great Library. I needed to find Uriel. I knew that if you ever wanted to find Uriel, he was usually in the library. However, it was a bit of a forbidden place, at least for me, anyway. It was the repository of all the knowledge of heaven. I was determined, in my belief, that Uriel could help me. Once I reached the library, I pushed through the large metal doors as shelves upon shelves of books climbed higher and higher to greet my view. The room's large bay windows were encased in dark red draperies, and golden lanterns rested on each mahogany table, lending a dark and ominous feel to the room. I saw Uriel hunched over one of the tables, writing in a very big book. He sensed me, and looked up in surprise.

"My Lady?" He exclaimed as he rose.

"I want to see the humans!"

"What?"

"Uriel, I want to experience what it is like to be human! I want to –
"

"Does your father know about this visit?" Uriel cut me off.

"No," I bowed my head in defeat. "I was with Raphael for my lesson."

"Let's go then," I heard him sigh.

He escorted me back to my teacher, who jumped up and rushed over upon seeing us enter the gardens. I was sure Father would be present too. Did he not tell Father was missing?

"Princess!" Raphael cried. "Why did you run off like that? Your Father would have my head if something happ-"

"What do you care? "I spat out, burying my face against Uriel.

"My dear, do you think I do not care for you, in only that you are my Lord's daughter?" He pulled me away from Uriel, encasing my hands in his. He then knelt to me. "I am sorry if I gave you that impression. You are dear to me, and you know that. You are my student." Raphael smiled softly as he pulled me into his embrace. It was then that I felt Raphael as he opened his soul to me. I felt his love and sincerity for me. Raphael did love me for me, not because he was obligated or commanded. I closed my eyes, absorbing up this love. I shared loved for him too, for he was my teacher, and I always wanted to make him proud of me. "So much like her..." I heard his thoughts whisper. Who was I like? Abruptly our connection broke as Raphael pulled away. "How about we go to my chambers now? I will make you some of my soothing tea, maybe even divulge my secret recipe too," he winked. I smiled and nodded as we headed to his chambers. I sat on the all too familiar white cushioned, golden chaise as Raphael went to prepare his famous tea. After a little while, he came back in with a golden tray with two cups. He set the tray on his desk as he picked up a cup proposing it to me, to which I took kindly. The tea smelled good as I closed my eyes, just inhaling the sweet tea aroma. "Soothing tea for the troubled soul?" Raphael said as I opened my eyes.

"Is my soul troubled, Raphael?" I felt his ambient joy fall down a notch as he knelt in front of me.

"So serious today," he said as he brushed a piece of fallen hair from my face. "You, tell me. Is it?"

"I don't know," I said, looking down at my cup of tea again. I could not voice about the darkness I felt lurking in my heart. How the voices whispered, they all must die. How I felt so overcome...I just could not.

"Let's learn now and shake this gloomy mood, shall we?" Raphael said, rising as if he felt my bubbling turmoil. "If your father asks what you have learned today, what will we say, huh?" I then knew what I wanted to do.

"Can you help me with something?" I said, looking back up at him. "I want to make a gift for someone. I..um had kicked one of Fathers Elite Guards, and I want to say sorry to him." I smiled sweetly.

"So, I heard," Raphael replied, arching a brow as he took the cup from me, putting it back on the tray. "I have just the thing. "he grinned, then went to put the tray away. When he came back into the room, he sat beside me. "How about making a healing stone? You take a stone and put a little of your healing essence into it. He can heal minor scrapes and bruises like the one you gave him, which I am sure he is probably still suffering from."

"Raphael!" I pouted, nudging him.

"Joking," he soothed, smiling. "Now, let's go find you a stone!"

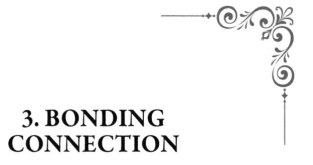

3. BONDING CONNECTION

To get our stone, Raphael took me deep into the forest within the gardens. We walked until we came to a clearing with a shallow pond in the center. Nudging me forward, I looked down into the clear water to see many multicolored stones resting at the bottom of the pond. I sank to my knees and immersed my hands in the water. I let my instincts take over, closing my eyes as I let my fingers graze across a smooth, warm stone, and I knew it was the one. I opened my eyes as my fingers gripped the stone, pulling it out. I turned back to Raphael.

"Raphael! I found my stone," I exclaimed jubilantly, rising to my feet running over to him with pride. Raphael looked down at me with a smile and stroked my cheek approvingly.

We returned to Raphael's chamber, where he showed me how to extract some of my healing essences to put into the stone. We decided to call it a day afterward, so he escorted me back to Father's chambers. I curtsied, thanking Raphael. He gave me another smile, then handed me the stone he had placed in a burgundy velvet pouch, taking his leave. Starting for the doorknob to go inside Father's chamber, I paused. I wanted to deliver my gift. I took a deep breath, clutching the burgundy velvet pouch to my chest, and headed towards the stairs to the lower levels. I knew this was bold of me. I wasn't supposed to go down there without Father. Hell, I never was allowed to wander anywhere alone; it was maddening! It would be quick, and Father would see no harm was done. Seriously, what could happen? As I reached the lower levels,

I stopped, surprised to see two guards talking in the hall some distance down. I clutched my pouch tighter to me as I headed towards them. I was relieved as I got closer, recognizing one of them being the copper-haired Elite guard that was with Pio.

"Um, ex-excuse me," I said as I reached them and curtsied.

"Ah, and there she is. We were just talking about you, and my, my you've grown," he grinned as his honey-colored eyes scanned me up and down. "Amazing," he breathed as he sauntered closer to me, examining me all over with his eyes. Okay, so maybe this was not a good idea. I did not like his gaze all over me. I took a step back and he instantly caught me, grabbing my wrist. I pulled away hard, stumbling back as hands caught me. I looked up behind me to see it was Michael.

"What do you two think you are doing?" Michael said, speaking directly towards the guards. He then crouched down, putting his finger to my lips. "Shh, little miss, you are safe now." My eyelids suddenly grew heavy as I could not keep my eyes open, and everything was gone.

"Michael! Michael!" I heard Father's voice boom with concern.

"I found her, my Lord!" Michael called, and I felt him scoop me up in his arms. Oddly, I was completely unconscious, but my brain was very aware and could listen to them perfectly.

"My daughter!" I heard Father cry out.

Then I heard another concerned voice. "Is she okay?"

It was Pio!

"She'll be fine," Michael said. "Just a little too much excitement. It seems, though, she did come all this way for you." Michael said, stressing the "you."

I felt him take the pouch from my clenched fingers as the unconsciousness crept up deeper into my mind. I gave in, letting it take me under into a peaceful sleep.

When I awoke, I found myself in bed. I sat up to see Father sitting at the foot of the bed. "Father?"

"You're in your chambers," he said. "This is where you will sleep and stay. Since you think you're so big, and you can roam the tower alone, a guard will be posted outside your door."

"Father." I winced when someone knocked on the door.

"Seems you have a visitor already," Father said as he rose to open the door. One of Father's Elite guards was there; the blonde one that I discovered was named Kyi. It was not Pio for which I was slightly disappointed. Kyi bowed to Father as he walked over to me.

"Pio thanks you for the gift. He wished he could have come by himself but had to do some work for your Father." he said, giving Father a glance for approval. Father nodded.

"Thank you. "I said, bowing my head.

"Rest some more now, and enjoy your chambers."

Father smiled, motioning around the room. "I put some earthly gems I thought you might like on your vanity. There are also some linens and silks in your wardrobe. Maybe we can design you a new dress. You are not to venture out anymore, you understand?" Father said sternly.

"Yes, Father." I said, glancing back up at him.

"Good."

I looked up to see Father leave along with Kyi. I sighed as I took a look around me; the room was now lavishly decorated in reds and gold that I found myself liking a bit more from the awful childish pink. Michael had done what he said he was going to, as I looked at my vanity table to see a now flawless mirror. So now, this was indeed a glamorous prison.

That night, Father released me from the dungeon. The two of us sat outside Father's balcony, viewing the majestic night while sipping some of Raphael's healing tea. I decided to be bold once again. It seemed I was on a roll. The precious humans awaited me, so I asked Father. "Father...can you tell me more about the humans?"

Father looked over at me in surprise. "Why do you ask?"

"They fascinate me so-"

"You are still very young; do not worry about the humans." Father scoffed, looking back out into the night. I dropped the subject as I took a sip of my tea in silence. The humans were much like us, with a beauty not so unlike our own. Only the ancient ones had the androgyny porcelain beauty to them. I wanted to be human. I knew it could be done. As a human, I knew I could be free.

Freedom always has a price, though.

4. WATCHER

The day began in the grand audience chamber, where everyone waited for the heavenly politics to commence. Music was provided, to which I contributed my vocals along with two other female angels. It was then that I saw him again, Pio. Our song ended when he entered through the large metal doors with the rest of his entourage. The appearance of Father's Elite Guards signaled the start of the council meeting. The three walked up to Father, who sat on his throne with the heavenly council surrounding him. They bowed to him and I saw Pio glance back at me. I immediately averted my gaze, looking down at the floor. Was I staring at him so much that he could feel it? I peeked again under my lashes to see him smiling as his gaze turned back to Father. I, then, got nudged as we were to take our seats in the side stands of the auditorium. As I took my seat, I heard gasps all around me. I looked over and saw Pio sitting down next to me. His two comrades sat by us as well.

"It's been a long time; you have grown a lot," he said as he turned his deep blue eyes on me. I was silent.

"Don't you remember me?" he smiled. "I'm Pio. Nice to meet you," he said, extending his hand. I threw myself into his arms.

"I'm so sorry! I..." I trailed off as blackness started to consume me. Another one of Father's rules was that heavenly politics were not to be of my concern.

"Um, Father..." I heard Pio say in his mind. "*It's okay, my son.*" I heard Father respond through their link. "*The worst she can do is drool on you.*"

Pio chuckled. "Thank you, my Lord."

I awoke to the council meeting being over and still in Pio's arms.

"Morning, sunshine, let's meet your Father. It's over now," he said, smiling. We rose and walked over to Father as others left the chambers around us.

"So, you used one of my guards as a pillow, huh?" Father said as he crossed his arms over his chest, looking down at me, trying to act stern.

I looked down shyly. "Yes, he's warm like you, Father." Father busted into a booming laugh as he gathered me into his arms.

"I guess that is somewhat true. I did create him!"

"Father, was I created?" I felt Father's emotions pale for a moment, which puzzled me. He then turned to thank Pio and he wished him luck on his mission. Pio bowed, then turned, taking his leave. I watched after him, then looking back up to Father, I asked, "He is leaving?" Father smiled as he let me go, meaning he gave permission. It didn't matter that Father didn't answer my question as I ran after Pio. Catching up with him, I picked up his walking pace. Looking up at him, I asked. "Can you play?"

He stopped as he looked down at me and smiled. "Sure."

I took his hand as I dragged him out into the gardens. "So, you're leaving?" I asked simply as we took our spot under a large tall tree.

"Yes, I was one of the chosen."

"To go down there?" I asked. "That was what the council meeting was about, right?"

"Thought you were asleep?" He said, eyeing me suspiciously. "And the answer is yes, I am to be a Watcher. You see, your Father just wants to know how all his children are behaving."

"I've always wanted to go down there."

I sighed, raising to my knees and tucking my legs underneath me. "You don't like it here?"

"I do," I said, looking down. "It's just I don't get to venture out much, and Father said I am still young and not to get headstrong."

He chuckled. "You, headstrong?"

"I can be headstrong! Wait..."

He laughed. "Guilty as charged."

"Hey! "I pouted. I then laughed along with him.

"There you are, little miss. It's time for your lesson with Raphael."

I looked back behind me to see Michael standing there. He inclined his head. "Pio."

"Michael," Pio said in response. I rose obediently and started to walk to Michael but stopped. I glanced back at Pio, not wanting our time to end. He smiled, rising to his feet.

"It's been a pleasure," he said, walking over to me. "We must do it again sometime."

"But you're leaving."

"I'll have to come back and visit," he said as he knelt to me. I threw myself into his arms again, and I felt his arms wrap around me tightly. His warmth was so wonderful. I felt safe. No demons could reach me if I was in this place. I had to let go, though, and I let Michael take me to my lesson with Raphael.

"MY LORD!" I AWOKE THE following day to the sound of the guard yelling. I heard my food tray clatter to the marble floor. Quite a wake-up call, I grumbled and grudgingly sat up, catching a glimpse of my hand, which was no longer that of a child. My fingers were long, slender, and elegant. I ripped off the covers to see a pair of long and slender legs beneath me, then grabbed at my chest to feel the soft, supple form of full breasts. My door then burst open, revealing Father and Raphael entering as their mouths drop open at the sight of me. Raphael coming to his senses, steps forward, grabbing the sheet off my bed, wrapping it around me and scooping me off the bed to go with him.

"I will take her to my chambers, my Lord," he said as he walked past a very worried Father.

"What did I do?" I finally asked as we moved swiftly down the halls.

"Nothing, princess... Well...um, this was unexpected, yet expected," he chuckled. We arrived at his chambers, and he ushered me inside, closing the door quickly behind us.

"Raph-"

"Shush," he said, placing a finger on my lips. "I need silence." He removed his finger before starting to pace the room. I moved to sit on the chaise, watching his back-and-forth movement as he glanced at me occasionally. Finally, we got the signal that we could return to my chambers. As we returned, Father was still there, and I found my room had been completely rearranged, with a brand-new wardrobe filled with beautiful, new dresses for my new shape.

"Come in now," Father said as two female angels dressed in long hooded lavender robes entered.

"These are your assistants. They are to assist you in bathing, dressing, anything you need. There is also a guard outside so that you will not be disturbed unexpectedly." Father opened his arms, and I went into them. He embraced me tightly, then let go. "Beautiful creation," he said, smiling and stroking my hair. I smiled, and he returned it grander before exiting.

"Is there anything we can do for you, Milady?" I heard a soft voice say. Gods, I had forgotten my assistants!

I turned to them. "Um...bathing, please." I smiled.

"We will prepare a warm bath for you, Milady," one of my assistants said and they both bowed. After bathing, I wore a lovely off-shoulder rose-colored gown that hung slenderly on my new form. I thanked my assistants, dismissing them for the night and they left through a secret passage. I sighed, deciding I wanted to go to the gardens. I opened my door, peeking out, seeing the guard at his post as Father said outside my door. I opened the door, further, stepping out.

"May I go to the gardens?" The guard turned around and smiled upon seeing me.

"Of course, Milady," he said.

I made the motion for him to lead. "Shall we proceed?"

The guard chuckled to himself as he led the way, shaking his head. I followed behind him for a moment, then stopped, and he continued walking. I smiled, gathering up my dress, then made a mad dash the other way to Father's chambers. How gullible were these angels! I knew Father would not be in his chambers at this time as I soundlessly slipped inside, going straight to Father's looking glass so I might gaze down at my humans. I saw the children that I had watched before were still children, which saddened me. I knew, though, Heaven's and Earth's time was far different. Instead, I decided on watching the fully grown humans, which I was now. I loved them instantly, fascinated with the make-up, dresses, and jewels the females wore and how it made the males look at them, more entranced to pursue them into coupling. It was all enticing! Their children came from this union too! Could angels do this? I was addicted to the thought. What it would be like to touch another, to feel...to kiss...

"Are you allowed in here? My stomach dropped as I turned and saw the red-curls angel. It seemed like ages since I last saw her. She looked different to me now. We were now equal. She wore a slender gown of beige silk that further enhanced her red mane when she asked again, "Are you allowed in here?"

"Will Father be mad? I just- I crave to see their world," I said, looking back at Father's looking glass. She chuckled, taking a seat on his bench next to it.

"Are you sure you want to go down there? It's not all that it seems."

"You have been?" I exclaimed as I sat at her feet. "Tell me about it! I do want to go down there so much sometimes it hurts!" Despite no longer being in child form, I did seem to hold onto my childish ways. I looked away shamefully when I felt her stroke my hair lovingly, and instinctively, I laid my head on her lap. Such familiar emotions flowed through me. I wondered if this was what it felt like between a human mother and child. Father created us though, she was not my mother...right? I felt the heaviness of unconsciousness creep up on me. I gave into it willingly, not wanting to face these emotions. I knew this was Father's doing too. He had been alerted, and I had been caught; I would not fight.

PIO

The duty of a Watcher was to do just that: watch. We were not to interfere with daily human life, and we were not to be seen. This reminded me of the Watchers of old and how they failed miserably with that. Moreover, it reminded me that we are all susceptible to temptations of the flesh, whether human or angel. While most angels have openly taken a lover or two from Heaven, for me, the idea of coupling did not appeal to me much. Seeing this moved my dear friend Razz into a slight madness. Why did I have no interest in the female gender or in having a lover? It wasn't that I had no interest; it was that my work kept me busy. Razz still tried to hook me up with a female. Finally, I accepted the latest young female from his "Bon appetit" menu to get him off my back. Grabbing the female's hand, I dragged her off away with me. When we were safe from Razz, I let go of the soft hand I was holding as I turned to look at her and saw she was quite beautiful. She wore her tight, curly dark hair up, with tendrils falling down to frame her oval face; her soft violet eyes looked at me breathlessly.

"I'm sorry," I said, furrowing my brow as I stepped away from her. She smiled as she spoke, her voice sweet as an angel's voice should be.

"It is okay...my name is Ne'nel. It's just... I am the one Razz has always tried to offer you. It was always me. I wanted you to know that," she said, looking down coyly and twirling her fingers. "You are appealing to me." She looked back up at me flirtatiously.

"I am sorry, but I cannot." She looked at me puzzled as I cupped her face in my hands. "My duty is to our Lord," I said. I let my hands slip away, and I walked away, this was all I could give her. So, if that incident didn't quell my fear of giving in to the desire of the flesh on Earth, then it was simply a sign that I denied the truth. Someone else had my interest. I had not been on my mission for a day when I got the notice to return home. Obediently, I returned reporting to Father's chambers, suspecting only to find him there, but to my surprise, there was someone else. I didn't know her, but I knew of her as she sat on the council with Father. She had the most fiery red curls that made her stand out amongst the rest, so it was hard not to know of her. She sat regally in a deep, plush red velvet chair that almost perfectly matched her hair color. The slender gown she wore openly showed that she was very much a female. The androgyny of the council robes no longer hindered her. I nodded to her. "My lady." I bowed to Father. "My Lord,"

"I know you do not like much of the politics, Pio."

"Yes, my Lord, but-" Father raised his hand. "Home is not as it was, Pio, and loyalties seem to be in question. I know yours is unwavering, without a doubt. I need you to watch over her, Pio, to protect her. You are the only one we can trust." I glanced at the red-curled angel, but she remained expressionless. "You know of my newest, correct?" Father said, bringing my attention back to him.

I winced a bit, "Yes," I replied.

"Her name is Aye and-"

"She is mine," the woman proclaimed.

I looked at her stunned, then looked to Father, then to her again. How? Was this even possible for us? To... to...procreate?

"Yes, what she says is true," Father said tiredly, calming my thoughts. "Thus, Aye is unique, with untapped abilities others may covet and manipulate and use against us. So, we want to keep her safe." I was then told the sordid tale of how Aye came to be in our presence.

Aye's Story

In the beginning, Father created all. What was not written was that his siblings were also fascinated by the creation idea. First, Father created the heavens, and it was good. Next, he had his first children, the angels. One sibling, however, became jealous of these "angels." Likewise, he would try to create, but destroy them because they didn't measure up to his brother's' perfection. How did he do it? Also, why give these creatures free will? Did Yahweh even realize the drastic consequences that this could have! Father then created another angelic being. This creation was quite different from what Father had made before. Shapely and smaller than the others, it possessed an attractive look with long, flaming red hair. It was also said that Father hid his secret to creation in it. It was at this point that Father's brother decided he had to have her. Father shouldn't have all the glory. He would also prove giving these creatures free will was a mistake by seducing one of Father's stoic creations. His prize, Michael. He succeeded, as Michael was foolishly swayed to help him create a being that was something of semi-worth for him. Still, this creation was not perfection, as his brother's, but it would do, and it would serve with no will to its own, as it should be. Still, he wanted the red haired one. Gods, how that beautiful creature enticed him! He used Michael as his ears inside the tower, waiting until the time was right to pluck her. Sadly, he succeeded in his quest, kidnapping her while she was on a mission outside of Heaven for Father. But he found nothing, no matter how much he tortured and degraded her. Oh, and he loved degrading her. It was his pleasure though *he never laid a hand on her. He was, instead, using his semi-worthy creation to do it all for him. He loved to watch, though! It was not his fault! His brother should not have made such a succulent type of creature! He decided to check in on his pretty little red-head one night, finding her sleeping beautifully in the small cage he kept her in. He turned to leave, then stopped. He heard tiny little voices talking! What was this? He turned back around, walking closer to the cage and he reached out mentally to these small voices.*

"Hello, there."

"Hi!"

Gods! they replied to him! He gripped the bars of the cage, realizing the voices were coming from inside of her! Unbelievable! Never did he think! She conceived! She created! She was the key! Not only did she carry one creation, but two creations! One was male, and the other female like her. Either way it was perfect! They would be his new breed of perfection. The start of his army! He reached out to the tiny life forces again. "She belongs to you, my little son," he whispered to the male. "Watch out for your sister; she will be your bride one day. You are a new race, and your race will flourish! We will overthrow Heaven!" Oh! He was going to be a grandfather, how precious! The male child was born already twisted to their side and cause. The female child was born innocent. The flame-haired angel, fearful for her daughter's innocence being corrupted, resolved to escape. She ran away with Aye, returning home. Of course, Father accepted the child, but then his brother bombarded through the tower gates demanding the girl-child be returned to him. Father told his wayward brother no, instead setting a wager. We got to keep Aye, that is until she changed. Father's brother smiled, wholeheartedly agreeing, neither denying the dark destiny the child was created for.

I was told Aye knew nothing of this, and it was to stay that way. She must never know the truth.

"Why?" I asked out of the blue.

"To know her truth now could destroy her. We could lose her. I had one daughter nearly destroyed; I will not have another.. "Father stressed.

"Ignorance is bliss then."

"Indeed," Father said directly. "One thing we know for sure: Aye is a powerful empath, so be wary of her emotions. They can sometimes overwhelm her. Even love could be a dangerous emotion for her."

"Love?" I said, wondering what Father was implying.

"Aye is a new breed of angel, one we do not know much of. Other than that she has matured at a fast rate all her own. So far, though, she thrives on eating. She needs her nourishment three times a day on the dot."

I didn't ask any more questions. "As you wish, my Lord."

My whole existence shifted at that moment. Now my duty was to protect her. While I reported to our Lord how Aye was fairing, I was also reporting to her mother; thus, the trim on my uniform would change from gold to maroon to represent this allegiance. If anyone questioned, they would know who I worked under. And my first duty was to dine with her later that evening. Father said she was asleep in his private chambers and to take her back to her chambers till she had awoken. Once evening chimed, I headed to his chambers, walking in on a stunning scene. There they were, mother and daughter, and Aye was amazingly fully grown. Her head rested on her mother's lap like an innocent child who had fallen asleep at their parent's feet. The red-curled angel looked up to see me.

"Take her," she said as she looked down at Aye one last time, stroking her hair softly. "This soothes her by the way."

"I will remember," I spoke. She gave a slight smile, not taking her eyes off her daughter. She allowed her hand to drop to her side as I walked over and gathered up Aye in my arms to carry her back to her chambers.

AYE

I awoke to find myself back in my chambers as I sat up in bed, seeing Pio sitting on the floor resting against the end of my bed. My heart leaped at the sight of him. He had come back! He had kept his promise! I gathered my legs under me, crawling over to the edge of the bed peering down at him. I wondered if should I wake him. I cautiously reached out, tapping him on the nose. He jumped up awake, spinning around.

"I grew!" I smiled, holding out my arms.

Pio glowered, "And you're still a child. Get dressed; we are dining," he grumbled as he got up, straightening himself out, then walked out. Dressing in a flowing gown of dusty rose pink with long slit sheer off-the-shoulder sleeves. I walked out of my chambers, finding him standing there leaning against the far wall. He glanced up at me, then looked away, a bit disturbed as he pushed himself off the wall.

"Let's go," he muttered as he started off. I followed, noticing we were heading for the lowered levels. I paused, wondering if this was okay.

"We have your father's permission," he spoke, reading my mind. I nodded as he looked back at me, taking my hand, and we headed down the stairs. Once we reached the bottom, we headed to the left instead of straight, arriving at Pio's chambers. He opened the entryway escorting me inside to discover he had a dazzling table spread of nourishments set out on his beautiful veranda. His chambers were smaller in size than the upper chambers, but the openness of the veranda made it seem spacious. All he had for furnishing was a large dark wood bed that rested against the far wall next to the veranda and a desk that sat next to the entrance to his bathing room. I had never been in another's rooms before, well besides Raphael's and Father's. We crossed over to the table as I coyly ran my finger along the etched wood frame of the chair.

"You came back," I said.

"I said I would," he said as he took his seat in his chair. I took my seat as well as not being able to contain myself anymore.

"So, what was it like?" I asked eagerly.

"What was what like?"

"Down there?"

"Can't tell you that," he smiled.

I glared at him then started piling food on my plate a bit angrily. Once my meal ended, he escorted me back to my chambers. When we arrived at my chambers, he took my hand.

"Thank you for your presence, Milady," he bowed.

"Thank you, too. "I said as he looked up at me with those beautiful deep blue eyes. He gave a slight smile, then kissed my hand, letting it go as he took his leave.

"Was my daughter on a date?" I heard Father's voice tease coming up beside me. I looked over to Father as he put his arm around me, squeezing me. He chuckled. "Did you have a nice time?"

"Yes, Father. "I said, embracing him back warmly.

FATHER'S SCHEDULE HAD begun to become increasingly demanding, which led to our time together less and less. Father had now given up on posting a guard to watch over me after I had managed to easily slip away from each one to go human gazing. I felt a bit sorry for those guards, for I am sure Father was displeased that I had managed to escape his supposedly abled guards. Instead, Father made me promise that I would not venture off human gazing again. I swore

Father was trying to kill me with boredom. My lessons with Raphael had even stopped. So, was I an official healer then? I then wondered if a healer could heal could they kill as well? Is this why there was the binding oath that no blood shall ever stain a healer's hands? It seemed logical that life and death went hand in hand. I wandered out into the gardens with these thoughts on my mind. Out in the gardens, the plants, the trees, they were my only companions really in this precious life of solitude in the tower. The pain of this solitude started to creep back up inside me. I felt like I was some sinister secret, a living sin in Heaven. Father would surely disagree. He pleased me with everything I desired, but what I wanted most was freedom to roam, to fly! I was an angel that could not fly! The willow tree lifted her branch up, brushing her soft leaves against my cheek. I smiled as I caressed her leaves, back thanking her for the concern. I crouched down, parting her branches as I crept underneath to rest against her trunk, staring up at her canopy of branches above me. I closed my eyes, letting my mind start to drift.

"*Kill them....*" Ah, my sweet seductive whisperer was back. "*Don't you want to see their blood flow!;To taste it!*"

"Yes..." I breathed as luscious hunger lust rose inside me.

"My Lady!" I jumped, opening my eyes. I rose, coming out from under the canopy of branches to see one of Father's messengers.

"Your Father requested you, and you did not answer."

"I... must have fallen asleep," I smiled...and lied.

"Well, I am here to escort you to him." I gave the nod and smiled as we left the gardens together. Why did I not hear Father's call?

That night I decided to shower out in the waterfalls to cleanse my body. My mind. My soul. I was still haunted by what happened by the tree. I slipped off my robe, venturing into the cool waters that encompassed the falls. I paused, sensing somebody was watching me.

"So, are you, my guardian, now?" I remarked slyly back over my shoulder.

"In fact, I am," Pio said, stepping out from the shadows. "Let's go. We're meeting your Father for dinner."

I looked after him, confused. What did he just say?

I returned to my chambers, dressing in the new slender gown of cream-colored silk with off-the-shoulder pearl straps that Father had set out for me to wear. I wore my hair pulled up intertwined with pearls as well. I followed Pio as we walked to Father's chambers, where an elegant feast by candle light was set out. My mind mainly drifted through dinner, only occasionally picking at my nourishment as Father and Pio talked.

"So, what do you think, my child?" I heard Father's question, pulling me out of my

thoughts. During their talk, one thing I heard quite clearly was Pio was now my Guardian, my "Watcher," you could say. I resented this a little, Father still thinking I needed a babysitter.

5. FIRST DAYS

"Wakey, wakey," I heard an all too familiar voice say. Oh, so now, since he is my Guardian, does this make him my personal alarm clock too? I pulled the covers over my head.

"Your bath has been warmed and is ready, my lady. While you bathe, I will fetch your nourishment."

I peeked from under my covers slowly to see him exit. Curious, I got out of bed and went into my bathing room, seeing all the essentials I needed for bathing laid out for me, which made me more curious about him. After bathing, I returned to see a dress laid out, all ready for me to wear. When had he done this? Had he chosen this for me? I slipped the dress on over my head only to somehow become entangled. I cursed him for choosing this dress for me to wear. This could not be happening! I froze, hearing my chamber door open and I soon felt hands on my body helping me out of my predicament. Once I finally got out of my entanglement and into my dress, Pio tied the back of the corset on the rustic red-colored gown and I slipped the straps up onto my shoulders.

"Thank you." I said, a bit embarrassed.

"Here, sit." he said, motioning to my vanity table. I looked at him a bit confused but obeyed, sitting at my vanity table, I noticed the tumble mess of my hair. I watched as he picked up my brush and started running it through my hair gently. I did not expect this of him. I thought, as Father's Elite Guard, he would be hard and cold. All of Father's soldiers were.

"Shall we eat now?" I heard him ask, bringing me out of my thoughts. I rose, walking over to the table that had been set up in my room for my nourishment. I sat down as Pio brought over the tray of food, setting before me a lovely selection of fruits. Famished, I dug in as Pio sat down across from me. It seemed I was the only one that required daily nourishment in the tower. I did not know why, but I never questioned it. I liked eating.

"Your day is free, except your father requests our presence for the next time you need nourishment."

"Okay." I mumbled with a mouth full of food.

"Such a lady." he said, arching a brow.

I swallowed. "Haha, very funny." After, nourishment, I asked to go out into the gardens, so he escorted me there, allowing me to lead the way. I guessed he had been forewarned on my talent of slipping away, plus he was one of Father's elite. I was sure nothing could get past him. We entered the gardens with the waterfalls where I had bathed the fateful day before. I sat on the rocks by the falls gathering up the skirt of my dress as I dipped my toes in the water. I looked over to see Pio leaning against a tree with his arms folded across his chest, watching me. I turned back to the water and I started to hum a tune. I suddenly felt a warm hand grip my shoulder. I looked back to see it was Pio.

"Stay with me."

"What?" I asked, confused.

"I thought that was my little miss singing." I saw Pio wince as I looked beyond him to see Michael had entered the picture. It would be a welcome enjoyment. Please continue; we could use a change from those angelic choirs singing all the time." Michael chuckled.

"We should go back to your chambers." Pio said curtly as I looked back up at him.

"But I do not want to go back."

"Now." he demanded, stepping closer to me so only I could hear. "Or I will carry you over my shoulders! Please," he softened. I sighed, offering up my hand for him to take in defeat. He took my hand as I swung my feet around to the dry ground and stood. We left the gardens, passing Michael as he moved aside and bowed. I glanced back at Michael as he looked up, smiling at me. As handsome as Michael was, he was mysteriously strange too. When we reached my chambers, Pio opened the door for me to enter. I went inside as he followed in behind me, and I heard him close the door behind us. I glanced back behind me, then looked away.

"Can I be alone please, you can stand guard outside." I ordered. I then felt his warm touch on my shoulder again.

"I am sorry, I cannot." he said soothingly. I spun around to face him, angry. How dare he! Instead, I tossed myself against him and buried my face against his chest feeling tears threatening. Why am I doing this? I...I...disliked him! He was a jerk! I then felt him pull me away.

"Why don't you rest? Then it should be time to meet with your Father." I nodded my head as I went to sit on my bed. Pio came over and lifted my feet upon the bed as I laid down, curling up on my side to soon drift off.

Suddenly I jolted awake, surprised that I had indeed fallen asleep. I looked around to see Pio sitting on the floor against my bed, sleeping again. A sly smile curved on my lips as I crawled over to the edge of my bed to peer down at him. The next thing I knew, I was flipped overlaying on his lap, looking up at him as he laughed.

"Let me up!" I glowered up at him trying to pull myself off him. "I want to prepare for Father. Should we not be going?" He stopped laughing, taking my hand as he drew in closer, our foreheads almost touching. A strange heat rose to my face.

"Wrap your arms around me then," he said darkly. I obeyed without thought as I slipped my arms around his neck. He then stood up with me cradled in his arms.

"You're fine, let's go," he smiled as he walked us over to my door, hitching it open with his foot.

"Wait!" I cried as we walked down the halls with him still carrying me. "You know I can walk." He stopped, looking surprised.

"You can?" He smiled, squeezing me. "You know I like a strong woman."

"Pio!" I said as I felt my face warm again. I was not sure what this was, but I had wished he'd stop making me do it! He then set me down as I saw we were already in front of Father's chambers. He had carried me the whole way? Pio was about to knock when I just busted in.

"Father!" I exclaimed. Father was standing there with welcoming open arms, which I gladly ran into hugging him tight. I looked behind me to see Pio, still standing at the door, bowing.

"Come in, Pio, let us dine." Father bellowed cheerfully. We sat together as Father and Pio spoke about me and how things were going on his first days with him as my Guardian. Father then turned his attention to me finally.

"You know I want you safe. I cannot always be there, my child. Pio is with you at my wishes. Please understand that."

"Yes, Father." I complied. Our dining was finished and Father hugged me goodbye. Pio bowed to his Lord as we both exited his chambers.

"I want to go to the gardens." I said absently, starting to walk somberly

down the hall. Father wanted me safe, but from what? What if the danger was myself? Was that why I needed some protector? I felt the tears start to sting my eyes as I gathered my dress up and ran. I stopped when my tears blinded me, and I could go no further. I wiped my eyes with the back of my hand, seeing I was at the entrance of the garden. I stepped off the marble and out into the gardens wondering if Pio was nearby. It did not matter. I headed to the waterfalls untying the back of my dress, letting it slip off my body as I walked, reaching the waterfalls. I gazed into the pool, the falls cascading down. My heart ached.

"Ease your pain, child...come to us. Be what you were meant to be!"

I cocked my head. Was the water talking?

"*Yesss, come unto us.*" It purred, answering my thought. "*Let go of your restraints! It hurts you! Be free!*"

"Free?" I whispered. Those words caressed my heart so sweetly. No longer would the dreams; the voices haunt me. I knew it. I closed my eyes, stepping into the waters as I felt cold darkness rise up to consume me in a dark plume of blackness.

"Aye!" I heard Pio's voice cry. I opened my eyes slightly to see Pio looking down at me with such worry on his handsome face. He was so handsome with his dark wet hair dripping on my cheeks. I could not keep awake, though, as my eyes closed, disappearing him from my sight.

"Raphael!" I heard Pio shout as I started to awake again, seeing everything in a blurred red haze. I was so cold, so starving! It hurt!

"What the –" Raphael said, rising from his desk. "What happened?"

"I don't know. We had visited with her Father-"

"Lay her down," he interrupted. I felt myself being laid down as Raphael laid his hands over me. "Damn." he muttered.

"I feel I am being left out on something." Pio said. "Am I not her Guardian? Should I not be privy to know everything about my charge?"

"Fair enough." Raphael said. "Give me your arm."

Pio complied as Raphael manifested a blade, gripped Pio's arm, and sliced into his flesh. I felt a warm sweet liquid touch my lips. "Drink it, Princess, it's okay." I heard Raphael coo. I clutched the source the sweet nectar was coming from hungrily to me, suckling in all the sweet liquid I could get and it, soon, soothed me back into a lull.

"Pleasurable, isn't it?" I heard Raphael smirk. "That is what she is really feeding on, your pleasure. That, and they just have a nasty blood lust appetite." Raphael said, wrinkling up his nose. "We've seen her kind in action thanks to her brother. Remember, Aye was meant to be a killer and to kill us all."

"To be killed by beauty then." I heard Pio whisper.

"Then you are under her spell."

"No," Pio said. "I am her guardian, nothing more."

I AWOKE TO THE FEELING of being encased in an enormous warmth, so I nuzzled into it more. "Are you nuzzling me?" I heard Pio's voice underneath me. I opened my eyes wide, finding myself lying against Pio in his lap. I jumped up, sliding off his lap, and stumbling to my feet. How long had he been holding me?

"I was not." I said defensively.

"Fine, if you say so." he said as he rose, raising his hands in surrender. "You should get dressed then." he said, motioning me up and down. Again, the familiar heat rose to my cheeks. Ugh! The man was incorrigible. I stomped away to dress in a simple V-neck medium-length white dress with a red sash tied in the back. Still fuming in my mind, I tried to connect the sash behind me when I felt Pio's hands take over. The man confused me. He could be a sarcastic jerk one second, kind and gentle the next.

"Why do you have to be such a jerk?" I said exhaustedly.

"Well, I have been called worse, and by my own men too...."

I turned to face him, wondering if he was insane. "Don't you miss your former duties? Why are you watching over me? I-"

He took my face in his hands as my breath caught in my chest. "No, I do not. Your Father requested me, but I was honored he trusted me to do so."

"Thank you," I said, slipping his warm hands from my face. I then smiled sweetly, clasping my hands behind my back. "I am fine now."

Pio dropped his head wearily as he went and collapsed onto my bed.

"You're going to give me gray hairs now."

"Angels don't get gray hairs...do they?" I asked as I slinked myself back towards my door. Just as I turned to grab the knob, a hand instantly slapped onto my wrist.

"Oh no, you don't," he said as he slipped his arms around my waist, swinging me back around.

"Let me go!" I glowered, tugging at his arms around my waist.

"But you were nuzzling me before." he whined.

"I thought you were a pillow."

"No, you did not think I was a pillow." he smiled against my cheek.

"Okay! I didn't, you win." I said, giving up when there was a sudden knock on my door. We both looked up, surprised as he let me go. I walked over to the door, oddly feeling naked without his arms around me. I quickly shook that thought out of my head as I opened the door to reveal Raphael.

"How are you feeling, Princess?" Raphael beamed cheerfully.

"I am better, thank you." I curtsied.

"May I speak with your guardian for just a moment?" Raphael looked over at Pio, and I looked back to see Pio nod; he then walked out with Raphael and closed the door behind them. I crouched down, putting my ear to the door to listen.

"I'm fine, Raphael, thank you. I will do as our Lord requests. She is listening through the door, by the way." I gasped as the door swung open and out. I splattered onto the marble floor.

"Very well then." Raphael said. I looked up to see Raphael pat Pio on the shoulder with a weary look, and then he walked away.

I stood up and bowed before Pio. "I am sorry for listening!"

"You are an impossible girl, aren't you?" I winced as he put his finger under my chin, lifting my face to look at him.

"And you still like me, right?" I smiled sweetly.

He chuckled. "Yes, I do, though I cannot let this misbehavior slide." he scolded as I stood up strait-laced, a bit shocked.

"What?"

He intertwined his hand with mine and pulled me along to leave. "Father gave me permission to punish as needed."

"Father did not!" I choked.

A mischievous smile spread across his face as he looked back at me. "Let's go now, naughty girl."

When we approached the audience chamber, we found its doors wide open. As we walked in, Father stood alone, though two Elite Guards accompanied him, two whom I later learned were the copper-haired Sachs and the light blonde-haired Kyi.

"This is my punishment?" I asked a little too loudly and my voice echoed in the near-empty room. Pio turned to me as he put a finger to my lips.

"Shh. If you show you can behave through this, you are off the hook, okay? Can you behave?"

"Yes, sir." I breathed immediately.

"Good." he said as he kissed my forehead lightly. I watched him walk over to where Father was, he bowed to Father and then shook the hands of his men. Father then spoke. His voice trailed off as a growing ring filled my ears, causing me to wince as I covered them in pain.

"Father!" I grumbled to myself. I even had to be sheltered from this! Finally, the ringing stopped, and I saw Kyi bow to Father and shake Pio's hand. I did not need to hear that he was the new leader of Father's Elite Guards now since Pio was my Guardian.

"Now it seems my daughter is in need of some attention." Father said as he turned to me with open arms. I smiled as I ran to his loving embrace.

"Father!" I cried.

"Would you like to spend some time with me? Pio does have some business he should attend to." Father said, looking over at Pio. I looked back at Pio as well. I wanted to spend time with Father, but Pio...

"Yes, my Lord, I do." he bowed.

The other two guards bowed as well. "If there is nothing more of us, my Lord," Kyi said.

"Yes, you all may leave." Father replied.

PIO

"**S**o how is the babysitting going, oh former great leader?" Sachs teased as we exited into the halls.

"Fine, copperhead." I retorted. Sachs had the hair color of shiny copper, hence the nickname. Sachs smiled then bowed to us cordially.

"Well, I have some business to attend to, former great leader and new great leader." he said, nodding to Kyi. He saluted and we watched him jog off.

"Hasn't changed at all huh?"

"No, not at all. "Kyi chuckled, then looked at me seriously. "So, was this your idea?"

"What?"

"Come on, Pio, you know I am not our Lord's little favorite. The Elite Guards were in a stand still once you got promoted to babysitting."

"Well, I guess that was not the case, as our Lord had decided to keep the Guards intact. Who would do all my left behind paper work now that I 'm gone?" I grinned.

Kyi chuckled, "Ah, the truth comes out." Oh, yes, I had heard whispers about how others felt Father always favored me. I mean, not many would be able to stand up to Father the way I did. Sachs once tried to question Father and it wasn't pretty. Either way, I avoided putting my arm around my friend, ushering him along with me.

"Sadly, my old friend, my duty calls again. If you'll excuse me." I stopped, bowing gentlemanly to him, then saluted, jogging off, Sachs style. In truth Kyi was right, it was my doing. Father had wanted to disband the Elite guards but I had talked him into keeping them in service. I knew Father had done this for my sake.

I soon found myself in the gardens with waterfalls. Guess Aye's choice of leisure was rubbing off on me. I rested against a tree closing my eyes when Father paged me officially. No rest for the wicked it seemed. I met Father and Aye outside of Father's chambers. I watched as Father hugged Aye one last time before releasing her back into my care. I nodded to Father, then put my arm around Aye as I ushered her off with me.

"Pio, she is to see Raphael, please escort her." Father said silently.

"Yes, my Lord." I replied. I stopped our walk, turning to face Aye. "I am to escort you to Raphael's."

"Raphael's?" she questioned as if it would be torture to be apart from me again. The girl should not be liking me so much.

"You are still his student, are you not? He requests your presence." I said curtly.

"Yes." she replied, bowing her head as if she'd been scolded. Damn, to try and be distant and detached from her was impossible, too. I didn't want her to hate me. I lifted her chin up to look up at me.

"Call for me when you are finished. I will hear you." I said softly. I then put my arm around her, giving her a squeeze. "Now off to Sir Raphael."

She smiled and laughed as we walked to Raphael's.

WHEN WE ARRIVED AT Raphael's chambers, we found him outside, waiting for us. His appearance was a little disheveled, like he just tumbled out of bed. The joking question was with whom? Our great healer was quite known to be a lady's man. I kissed Aye's hand, bidding farewell. I nodded to Raphael and he nodded in return respectfully. I headed off, leaving them to their lessons when Raphael's silent voice stopped me.

"Pio, stay. Perhaps our little lesson could be insightful. Follow quietly and don't be seen. I left the door open waiting."

I turned back around seeing an open passage way up ahead.

"Well, I am one for learning." I smiled. I headed toward the passage way opening following it through until it opened into a large warehouse styled room filled with small wooden crate boxes. "What the hell?" I spoke out loud.

"Pio!" Raphael screeched in my head.

"Sorry." I winced.

"Inside these boxes are the emotions of Aye's mother. Pieces we've plucked out just to stop her pain..."

"Like mother, like daughter." I said in awe.

"Yes, Aye is very empathic. Even her own emotions can get the best of her. So, we've been doing the same with Aye. In case you are wondering why her demeanor changed after the waterfall event. She doesn't remember it."

However, I knew this all too well. Aye was never aware of her emotions, or if she was, she buried them deep only to have them come back to haunt her while she slept. Every night, she'd awaken screaming and I'd climb into bed next to her, pulling her into my arms, stroking her hair, and soothing her back to sleep. I often wondered what she dreamed about. Humans say talking often helps, so I asked one night.

"Care to talk about it?" I felt her stiffen.

"No."

"As you wish."

"Pio?"

"Yes?"

"I like you." she said as she nuzzled in closer to me.

I chuckled. "That is dangerous, you know."

"How so?" She said, looking up at me so innocently.

50

"That is for me to know and you to find out." I said, giving her a little smile. She gave me a chided smile as I chuckled again. "Rest now, my lady," I told her, stroking her cheek. She obeyed as she laid her head back down on my chest. Yes, this was dangerous indeed. I indeed was under her spell.

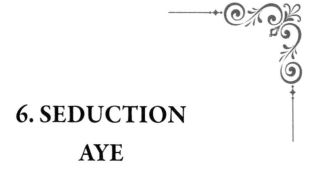

6. SEDUCTION
AYE

As time passed, restlessness set in both of us. However, noble Pio was not going to say a word. I wanted to do something other than playing earthly board games with Pio that Father had given me to quell my earthly fixation. Besides, I'd win every time, and I'm sure Pio did this on purpose. I would appreciate it if Pio challenged me once! It was then that I decided to challenge him. As usual, we were playing chess when I said I wanted to take a bath. Of course, he obliged me as he got up to prepare my bath. My sly little smile spread across my lips at that moment, as I dashed out the door making my way to Father's chambers to greet my humans. What did I hear after I exited Father's chambers?

"Got that out of your system?"

I cringed at the familiar voice sulking. Of course, I could not outwit the great Pio after all. In all respect he was Father's Elite guard to which I realized he had allowed my little escape. I smiled to myself a bit thinking it was kind of him to do so.

We headed back to my chambers and Pio opened the door for me.

"Bathe...for real this time and dress formally, then come back out." I looked down at myself in wonder at what was wrong with my appearance. "Just do it." Pio said, rolling his eyes. I obeyed, going inside my chambers to get clean and dressed. I knew exactly what I wanted to wear. Father had gotten it from a seamstress on earth.

"You went down to earth and shopped!" I remember squealing to Father.

He chuckled. "Yes, I guess I did. I saw it, and thought it would be lovely on you."

The dress was of crimson fabric that draped over one shoulder flowing down to the floor. It was accentuated with an embroidered gold high waist that I matched with gold arm bracelets, while leaving no adornments in my hair. As I looked in the mirror, I was amazed at my reflection. I was a woman now, yes indeed. I smiled to myself. No more was I going to be childish. Walking out in hopes that Pio approved of this as formal, I saw him standing there waiting with one foot propped back against the wall. He looked at me, then pushed himself up off the wall, looking away quickly.

"Let's go." He said curtly as he started off. Was something wrong with what I was wearing? I sighed as I gathered my dress up trotting after him. We came to the stairs that led down to the guard's levels. I almost stopped out of fear, but Pio was my guardian, so I put my doubts aside. We descended the stairs to the guard's level, following the paved corridor to his chambers. He opened the door to reveal a lovely little picnic set of food and wine set up on his veranda. I looked up at him puzzled. "Pio?"

He bowed gentlemanly. "I thought I would entertain you so you did not feel the need to run off again, and you haven't eaten yet, and neither have I."

He was going to eat? Out of all our time together I've never really seen him require nourishment. It seemed we dined mostly on the wine, though, which Pio said was from earth. I could see now how humans got addicted to this stuff.

"So, what are you thinking, my lady?" Pio asked, breaking the silence between us as we looked up at the night sky. "You are awfully quiet." I laid my head on his shoulder. "You trying to get fresh with me?" He said, arching a brow down at me.

"Pio...I do not feel well-" and I sicken in his lap.

"Then again maybe not." he said as I felt him lift my chin up to look up at him.

"I'm sor-"

He gave a sweet grin before rising to his feet and offering his hand. I accepted it as he assisted me in standing. He sat me down as we moved over to his bed. I raised my eyes to watch him enter his bathroom. He then reappeared, unbuttoning his soiled tunic. Heat began to rise in my face and I immediately averted my gaze. Nakedness was nothing to us, so why was my heart racing? Is it possible that it was the earth wine? I glanced back up at him from under my lashes to see him slip off his tunic. I stared at him...noticing how exquisitely created he was. I thought the human male form was pleasing, but he was... perfection! I quickly looked away again. What was I thinking? I then felt Pio take my hands and he pulled me up to stand. I closed my eyes, feeling his arms slip around my waist as he untied the back of my dress. The dress slipped off my body effortlessly to my feet.

"Can you walk?" His voice rumbled in my ear and my eyes flashed open. I looked down at my feet and took a step only to get tangled in my dress and I stumbled forward against him, to which he caught me in his warm embrace.

"Guess not." he said as he picked me up in his arms. "My, can't handle your liquor can you princess?"

"Pio..." I mumbled. I was so not in the mood for his sarcastic banter at the moment as my head nuzzled against the hollow of his throat, his scent filling my senses creating a burning hunger that wanted to devour him in delicious pleasure. He led us into his bathing room which was of pure pristine marble swirl. He stepped into the warm pool waters with me still in his arms. I wrapped my arms around his neck as he carefully laid me in the waters. He then stumbled a bit landing on top of me.

"Great," Pio said. "We're both going to pass out drunk and drown finding our naked bodies intertwined on top of each other." I laughed.

"You think that is funny?" He said pulling himself up to look down at me. "Father will bring us back to life just to scold us."

"I could heal us. "I said.

"Aww, but I was enjoying my drunken stupor." he smiled.

"I didn't know angels could get drunk.'

"I did not know either." he smiled again. Pio was truly beautiful with his deep blue eyes, yes like the deep blue ocean. He then started to lean closer and my heart stopped.

"Let's get out of here, I think we're clean," he whispered in my ear. He pulled himself off of me then offered me his hand to help me up. "Wait here; you can wear one of my robes." He exited, but quickly returned dressed in a white linen robe and he had another one draped across his arm for me. He held the robe up as I stepped out of the pool and into the awaiting robe. I tied it up with its sash and we headed back inside his chambers.

"Um...will you sleep with me?"

"What?!" Pio said looking back at me shocked.

"You won't lay with me while I sleep?" I asked, looking at him innocently.

Pio sighed as he shook his head. "I am sorry." he said, pulling me into his embrace tightly. "Of course, I will lay with you. I will hold you all night and protect you even in your dreams."

Little did I know the meaning of his words back then.

THAT NIGHT, I SLEPT peacefully; no nightmares haunted me. I woke the next morning to the sound of voices talking. I noticed Pio was gone from my side and I sat up seeing he was at his door. The top part of his robe hung at his waist letting me admire his toned muscular back. I scolded myself to stop with these thoughts!

"Pio?" I said scooting up on my knees. He looked back at me.

"WHAT? Saint Pio has a female in his room!" I heard another voice speak coming from behind the door. Pio focused his attention back to that person behind the door.

"It is not what you think."

"Sure, old friend!"

"Enough Razz you're frightening her!" Pio then slammed the door shut resting his forehead against it.

"You, okay?" I asked worriedly.

He turned his head smiling wearily at me. "Yes, thank you." he said as he walked over and sat on the bed beside me, taking my hand. "I will fetch you some clothes, and how about some nourishment?" I nodded. "Good then." he said as he let my hand go and stood up to leave. Suddenly my chest tightened in panic. I did not want him to go. I didn't want...

"Don't! I..." I choked, reaching out for him. I saw him look back at me worriedly. I dropped my hand, hanging my head in defeat. He pulled me into his warm embrace.

"Shh do not worry okay," he soothed. "I will be back soon." He then kissed the top of my head, letting me go. I looked at him, mustering a smile as he caressed my cheek with his thumb. I watched him walk out then closed my eyes taking a deep breath. What was wrong with me? What were these stirrings? I couldn't stand it any longer, I had to get out. I approached the door and paused. Pio would return with my nourishment and I was not to venture out on my own. I turned the handle; I did not care. I had to find Pio. Having reached back to the upper levels, I started to regret my decision. Here I was, un-presentable still in Pio's robes. This would go over really well if Father saw me. Plus, I did not know where Pio went to get my nourishment.

"Little miss?" I stopped looking up in surprise to see Michael standing in front of me. "Are you ditching your guardian?" he grinned. I looked away bashfully. That was not what I was doing. "You think it is fated we meet like this?" I looked back up at him confused. He reached out caressing my cheek. "So sweet just like your mother."

"Mother?"

"Ah," he tsked pulling away worried. "You were not supposed to know that yet little miss.," he pouted, then smiled as a jolting pain filled my body making it crumple down into white blindness...

"MICHAEL YOU SON OF A- "

I gasped, opening my eyes, finding my body was frozen.

"Nasty habit you've picked up from the humans Pio, you've been hanging with them way too much." I heard Michael say in the background. "You should be grateful I found her."

Michael? I'm in Michael's chambers? Why? *Forget little miss, it is our little secret.* I heard Michael's voice sooth in my mind. Unconsciousness crept back up to greet me as I gave in, forgetting. I wanted to forget.

I CAME TO, SEEING PIO lying sleeping beside me. My gods he was so beautiful to me. I often wondered, did he sleep at all in his duty to watch over me? I lightly brushed away a strand of his dark hair that had fallen on his face. I decided to bathe out by the waterfalls, I would not disturb him, he deserved to rest. Boy, I was never touching human wine again I thought. My mind thudded in a blurry haze. I soon reached the waterfalls, standing at the pool's edge, taking in a deep breath. I slipped my robe off letting it crumple at my feet as I waded into the pool toward the falls. Standing underneath, I let the showering waters consume me, cleanse me, then unleashed my wings, letting the cleansing waters cleanse them too. Erase everything like a bad dirty memory that I seem to have forgotten.

"What are you doing?" I looked behind me to see Pio standing there holding my robe.

"I needed to bathe. Are you mad?" I asked, closing my wings up back into my body. He didn't say anything as he stepped into the pool and reached me. He wrapped his arms around me from behind.

"I thought I lost you.," he whispered in my ear. My poor Pio; I ached to comfort him. I felt his worry, his fear. I turned to face him, reaching up to caress his face lightly with my fingertips as I had seen human women do to the ones, they felt affection for. I always wanted to know what it would be like to... kiss. I rose up on my toes as I pressed my lips against his. The taste of him was exquisite as I felt him respond, deepening our kiss, crushing me against him. He then scooped me up in his arms and he carried me into the hidden alcoves behind the waterfalls. So, our love affair began.

7. BLOSSOMING DAYS

The next day it was requested by Father to sing before the day's procession was to begin in the audience chamber. My stomach sickened, did Father know I was with Pio? I felt so sinful. Why me? Singing solo of all things?

"You're thinking too much again, you're going to overload," Pio said, tying up my sandal.

"What?" I said coming out of my thoughts.

He inched up my dress and kissed the inside of my thigh as my body quivered at the touch of his lips on my skin. I heard him chuckle as he pulled away.

"Sorry I won't excite you too much, and you will do fine my love.," he said as he rose to his feet then offered his hand gentlemanly. I sighed as I took his hand, rising to my feet. "Let's go now." he said.

We walked into the audience chamber as it was open and bustling with angels' starting to come in for the Heaven's council meeting. It was show time. Pio squeezed my hand and I looked to him. He nodded and I walked over to the little orchestra of angels. I wore an elegant backless halter gown of water color pink that cinched at the waist with a silver chain belt. My hair was in an elegant upswept pinned with my favorite silver comb Father had given me. I started my song as more angels entered for the meeting. As I neared the end like perfect timing, Father, and the heavens council walked in from the side stands, taking their seats as my song concluded its final note. Father took his seat then nodded to me. I approached Father high on his throne curtsying before him. I felt Pio's hand slip on the small of my back and I straightened. Father nodded to us both as Pio bowed then ushered us out together. Once outside I let out a breath, I didn't know I had held.

"Would you like to bathe and dress into a more comfortable attire?" Pio spoke, bringing my mind back into focus. I looked at him coyly biting my lip.

"Um...your chambers?"

He smiled. "Yes, that sounds nice, and as much as I like you wearing my robes, we will stop by your chambers and fetch you some clothes." I nodded seriously then smiled and we were off.

I STOOD IN PIO'S BATHING room staring at the bathing pool. I wondered what I was doing. I closed my eyes to feel Pio's lips graze my shoulder and his arms wrapped around me. I stiffened a bit, opening my eyes.

"Relax, it's not like we haven't been naked in a bath before." He grinned nipping my ear. He then moved to my neck, awakening my body's desire for him. How did he do this? He was all I wanted, all I hungered for. I wanted him to take me, possess me. I turned around capturing his lips with mine hungrily and he picked me up, taking me back to his bed. Afterwards, we laid together in the bathing pool, my head resting against his chest.

"Pio?"

"Hmm?" he asked, stroking my hair.

I lifted my head up to look into those deep blue eyes of his I so adored.

"If Father-"

"Don't think such things." he said, placing his wet finger against my lips. He then smiled mischievously as he leaned in and our lips met in perfect harmony. All thought was lost like I am sure he knew it would be. I did worry though; I couldn't help it. What about our love? Were angels supposed to love...like this? More so, were we? Pio's duty was to protect me, not love me. If Father knew, he would be furious.

PIO

A ye spent most of her time, now, in my chambers, which was fine with me. As well as watching over Aye, I got to finish up my endless paperwork. It was my responsibility to constantly report on Aye, particularly, if she showed any signs of changing.

"I must see Father." she said, suddenly rising off the bed.

"What?" I asked, looking up from my work.

"Father," she said blankly before running out of the room.

"Aye!" I shouted after her jumping up to give chase. Great, now I am going to have to apologize to my Lord that I sometimes cannot control his daughter. My footsteps caught up with Aye as she entered Father's chambers, so I followed in after her.

"I'm sorry my Lord -" I paused upon entering, seeing we apparently interrupted something. Father was talking closely with a cloaked female figure and I caught a glimpse of her bright green eyes that gave away, she was a Nephilim. What was their kind doing in heaven?

"It is alright Pio." Father said, bringing me back. "What is it my child?" Father inquired about Aye.

"I...um was wondering if we could spend time together, it has been so long Father...and does not Pio deserve a break from me?"

"It is agreed!" Father said.

"Father?" I blurted out stunned. At this time, I was not particularly concerned with formalities.

"You are released from your duties as a brief break. You may attend, or visit with a special someone if one is had." Father smiled kindly. I gave a tight- lipped smile, of course Father knew. I bowed to my Lord.

"Thank you, Father, I have none, but I do have some things that I do need to tend to." Aye looked back at me worriedly. "No pouting Ajo , it was your idea." I said in our private connection. Father and I were playing a game now. We both knew each other's hand, but none of us were coming clean. I had fallen in love with his daughter, and we both knew I had been warned. I could have any lover I wanted just not Aye.

I passed my time away from Aye in my chambers catching up on my paperwork. I wondered what Father and Aye were talking about in their time together. My last report to Father was on Aye and her nightmares. They had gotten worse, and deadly. She started to violently thrash in her sleep like a demon was trying to escape her. I tried to sooth her but her eyes then flashed open red to see the demon had won. We fought, and I have to admit Aye was a formidable opponent, but it was not her. I managed to subdue her by yelling my beloved nickname for her, in hopes of reaching her. She'd then wake no memory at all of what she had done. Father then messaged to pick Aye up, and I did just that, finding Aye in Father's chambers as Father said I would. It looked like they had been dining, when Father must have been called away. Aye was looking down at the humans again. She was dressed appealingly in a white Grecian styled gown, with gold rings that clasped at the shoulders and a gold linked chain belt that hung at her waist, her hair was elegantly pinned to one side. Okay, if Father wanted me to stop loving her, he had to stop dressing her so appealingly.

"Still fascinated I see," I said smiling and crossing my arms over my chest. Aye glanced back at me as she closed the looking glass and rose to face me.

"You are upset with me?"

"No, never" I said, crossing over to her. This was true. I never could be mad at Aye no matter what she did.

My chambers?" I said, stroking her cheek. She nodded and we headed back to my chambers as always.

"I am bored," she sighed walking into my chambers and releasing her hair from its pinned do.

"I am sorry Aye," I sighed as well, closing the door behind us.

"I want to fly." she said, gathering her dress up as she climbed up on my veranda railing.

"You are going to fall if you don't watch it." I said, coming up behind her.

"Then take me," she smiled daringly down at me. The temptress dared me. How could I resist?

"Let's go then," I grinned back as I started to unbutton my tunic, slipping it off. I offered her my hand, which she took, and pulled her down from the veranda catching her in my arms. I flared out my wings and we are off into the air. She clung to me tightly, burying her face in my neck as the wind whipped around us.

"You wanted to fly, yet you have your eyes closed?" She looked up at me.

"Yes! I just discovered I am an earth angel. Thank you!" She buried her face back against me as I laughed. I landed us on top of a large plateau and set Aye down on her feet. She opened her eyes immediately looking down at her feet enshrouded in plush green grass that was decorated with tiny white flowers. She looked around her to see the tower that she had once been chained to was nowhere in sight. She looked at me, and I smiled.

"What?" I grinned innocently and I saw the tears start to brew in her eyes. I reached out, caressing her cheek. "I love you." I whispered, stepping in closer as I leaned in claiming her lips lightly. She responded hungrily to mine and I felt my own hunger for her grow as we sank to the ground.

We quietly returned back to the tower at dark. No sooner had I set Aye down, torch lights lit up to reveal Father and two guards waiting for us. I felt Aye cling to me possessively.

"WHAT DO YOU THINK YOU ARE DOING TAKING MY DAUGHTER OUT OF THE TOWER!" Father boomed.

"Fa-", Aye started, as Father choked out her voice.

"GET HER OUT OF HERE!" Father called to the guards. A guard moved forward pulling Aye away from me, ushering her out of the room. An immediate meeting was called to decide on what should be done about my actions. I was held up in my chambers with a guard outside until my verdict was ready. They say Father is a loving God; some say he is a vengeful God. To tell you the truth he is both. To love him knows no bounds, and to fear him it is rightly so. When my chamber door finally opened, I was surprised to see the red-curled angel standing there.

"There is no judgment, you are free." She started to leave then stopped, glancing back. "Oh, Father wanted to see you, though." She then disappeared as the guard closed the door after her. Well, I was dumbfounded.

WHEN I REACHED FATHER'S chambers, I saw Father standing outside waiting for me.

"My Lord" I bowed.

"Pio- I understand you might have meant well by getting Aye out of the tower. I know also that she was in the safest of care as she was with you. Aye is in the gardens please go to her, you are her guardian only that is it."

"Yes, my Lord."

Following Father's orders, I headed out to the gardens to see Aye, and there she was sitting on the rocks by the waterfalls, her feet dangling in the pool. She wore a cream-colored, sleeveless medium length dress trimmed in red satin, that almost gave her a child-like appearance.

"So, your chambers or mine?" I said with a grin, sitting down on the rocks next to her.

"You are back?" She asked, still staring in the water.

"I never was gone. I am still your guardian, always. I just cannot guarantee I can obey our father's wishes." I said, slipping my hand in hers. She turned to look at me.

"Father forgive us."

"Father forgive us." I said as I leaned in, claiming her lips.

Please, Father forgive us.

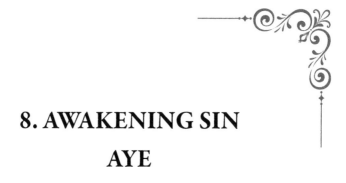

8. AWAKENING SIN

AYE

We had to stop this. I needed something to distract myself from ending up entangled in Pio's bed. The next day, I decided to take up painting, using the garden with my waterfall as my subject of art. Pio and I just could not be. I had never felt Father so furious before. I decided I would be cold and distant to him, that was it. My cold ice reserves melted, though, as I felt Pio caress a finger down the back of my neck making my body stir.

"My pardons." We both looked back behind us to see Pio's former comrade Kyi. Why was he here?

"What is it?" Pio said bluntly.

"My Lady," he bowed with a smile. "May I borrow a part of your guardian's time?" I was puzzled, but nodded to him. Pio caressed my cheek and looked up at him.

"I won't be far okay," he said, then kissed my lips lightly. Was Pio not afraid of showing he loved me? What if Kyi told Father? I turned back to my painting, but the passion was gone in it. I stood up dropping my paint brush as I walked over to the falls and sat on the rocks. I skimmed my fingers over the pool's surface.

"Little miss?" I looked up to see Michael standing there. "Out roaming alone again?" He smiled.

"No," I said looking back down at the water. "Pio is nearby."

"Do I make you uncomfortable Aye?" He asked, taking a seat beside me on the rocks.

"No," I said, adjusting to face him a bit confused. I wondered why he would ever think that?

Michael smiled. "I see now why our father adores you so," he said, taking my hand in his. A sweet floral aroma then whiffed around me. It was so soothing as I felt myself start to drift. I tried to speak. "Shh little miss." Michael cooed softly as his finger hushed my lips. He then whispered in my ear: "Don't worry, next time we meet I will be your lover then."

"Aye!"

I jumped, flashing my eyes open to see a worried Pio staring down at me. "Aye?" Pio said again as he helped me rise to my feet. "What happened? I called for you and you did not answer."

I did not know... wasn't Michael? I didn't remember.

THE TWO OF US RETURNED to Pio's chambers, where Pio went to prepare his bathing room for me. Wasn't there something I wanted to do? I had wanted to take up painting. Didn't I? What was missing? Pio took my hand calming my thoughts as he led me into his bathing room, where a large gold trimmed tub rested. I smiled. The tub looked earthly, like the one humans used to bath in. He then led me over to it to see it was filled with warm welcoming water. I felt him start to undress me, as I glanced back at him in amazement. Never in the beginning did I think he could be this loving, this gentle. He helped me slip into the tub, letting the warm water caress around me. I closed my eyes, relaxing. I wondered how he had gotten this amazing tub. Had he brought it back from earth? Just for me? I opened my eyes, sensing him still there. I watched as he began taking off his tunic then kneeled beside the tub, taking hold of my arm and started washing me. I looked at him in amazement again. He just smiled at me, continuing to wash me. Once done, he helped me out, then dried me. Afterwards we laid on his bed as he held me close against him. He stroked my hair and I started to drift into a lucid sleep.

"Michael!" I called out jolting up. I felt Pio instantly cradle me against him.

"Shh, he's not here, you're safe." Pio whispered, rocking me. Why did I say Michael's name? Pio laid me back down on the pillow. Without thinking, I reached up, touching his face with my fingertips. He took my hand and he kissed the inside of my wrist which made me instantly hunger for him. He caught on to my desire as he leaned down kissing my lips in a sweet kiss. I slipped my fingers through his hair pressing my lips to his more ravenously. I craved him, I hungered for him so madly. I wanted his passion, his soul. It fed me. Nourished me. I felt him succumb to my kiss as his lips replied in unison with mine.

"Damn," he muttered, pulling away. He pulled himself up off me as he went to grab one of his robes. "Your Father requests you. How am I going to explain the way his daughter is dressed, which is not?" he said, arching a brow at me tossing the robe onto the bed. I grabbed the robe solemnly slipping it on. "Let's go," he said. I dredged myself off the bed as he stood at the door motioning for me to go first.

When we reached the top of the stairs, sure enough, there was Father waiting along with two guards. I lowered my gaze, unable to look at Father, but then Pio spoke.

"She had one of her nightmares, said she was covered in blood."

Father lifted my chin up to look up at him. "Is this true daughter?" Father didn't let me answer. Instead, he pulled me into his arms holding me tight. "Well, we have to get you dressed appropriately if you are going to spend time with me." Father said as he let me go. He then put his arm around me as we walked off together, and I did not look back.

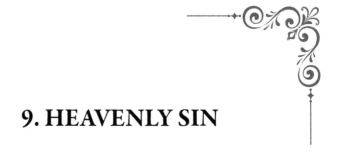

9. HEAVENLY SIN

Father did not say anything on why I was in Pio's chambers, still I knew he was suspicious. It was not that angels could not love, nor had lovers, many did. For me, though, it was apparently forbidden. Just like I was forbidden from oh so many things. After I had gotten in proper attire for Father, he took me to a special spot in the gardens. We came to a dead-end curtain of trees that opened up as soon as he arrived, revealing a faded white worn gazebo that made you wonder about its origins. What did it see so long ago in these gardens? Father walked towards the gazebo, and I followed and we both took seats on the paint chipped bench inside. I had decided to wear a slender halter dress of silver pearl that cinched at the waist. My hair was pulled up in an elegant upsweep intertwined with pearls. I glanced over at Father who just sat with his hands on his lap, starting at them. He then spoke. "I love you, my daughter."

"I love you too, Father." I spoke. I think everything was spoken in that moment though nothing much was said. Even if Father did not approve of our relations, he did trust Pio to the fullest to protect me. That was all Father wanted.

Once our time ended, we exited the gardens and I was released back into Pio's care once again. Pio and I walked down the halls silently until Pio finally broke the silence.

"We need to stop by my chambers first, then it is where ever you desire." Pio said, bringing me out of my thoughts. I winced at his words. Yes, this was the only way.

"Yes." I said solemnly.

We reached his chambers when he paused to look back at me.

"You can wait outside here, it will just be a moment." Pio said. I watched as he went inside. A painful tightness filled my chest. This was for the best. I was going to set him free. I started to grab for the door handle when the door opened.

"Aye?"

I threw myself into his arms. "Be with me!" I felt his arms wrap around me in his warmth as he kissed the top of my head.

"Aye," he sighed as I felt the torment battle inside him. I looked up at him and he closed his eyes, I felt his resistance breaking down. He grabbed my face, kissing me hungrily as we stumbled back inside his chambers.

I watched him as he slept peacefully afterward. I knew he would not be waking up so soon. I had drained his essence to the brink of unconsciousness. What was it that I had done though? Why did I play innocent with myself when I knew the truth? The voices, the dreams had all been right to my true nature. Now I understood why Father forbade us, ME of everything! How was I an angel? I craved pleasure! I needed it! It sustained me! I leaned down, kissing him one last time, Then, I dressed quickly, slipping out. I would tell Father I wanted a new guardian. Our love just had to die. I said this over and over in my head trying to convince myself of it all when a hand grabbed my wrist.

"LET ME GO! I DO NOT LOVE YOU!" I screamed breaking free to see it was Michael.

"Michael-?"

Suddenly, I was pressed against the wall as his lips came, crushing against mine. He then presses his forehead to mine, breaking the violent kiss. "How do I taste, little miss? I offer all of myself to you." I felt the insidious hunger rise, filling my vision in a lustful haze. I wanted him. I needed him. I slipped my fingers through his hair crushing my lips against his as his essence flooded into me; filling me. I was gone.

PIO

I awoke to Father's guard bursting into my chambers dragging me out of bed.

"You are wanted for interrogation for the attack on our Lord's daughter." One boomed as I was tossed naked, hitting into a cold stone cell encasing me in darkness. I laughed. Well, I had to admit I was impressed. Aye knew more than we thought. Damn! Why was she doing this! Breath, I told myself. I needed to calm my mind. I needed to figure out what was going on. Closing my eyes, I reached out with my senses searching the heavenly tower communications for my answer, which I found all too quickly. In fact, Aye and I were the talk of the tower. It seemed I had forced myself upon Aye. She had gotten away in which Saint Michael found her outside his chamber door disheveled, and battered, saying my name. How was I not surprised to find Michael's name was somehow in all this. There were questions on Michael, and his loyalty to us of late. Father would do nothing though. His only reply was if Michael was lost, he believed Michael would find his way back home on his own. Still could Father possibly believe all this? That I'd hurt Aye! I sighed cutting my connection. I must have fallen asleep because I jumped awake at the cell door opening to reveal a familiar figure I never thought I'd see.

"You are to report to your Lord. He is in his mission's room chamber. There are clothes for you outside." Gabriel said, jutting his head.

I chuckled to myself as I started to rise. It was good to see Gabe again.

I entered into Father's mission's room and its welcoming red velvet decor. To which, I was surprised to see Aye sitting on the floor next to Fathers throne like she was his little pet.

"Pio," Father's voice boomed, bringing me back to focus. "I am assigning you down to earth on a private mission. Get the job done the best way you can, no worries of diplomacy understood?"

"Yes, my Lord." I complied with obedience. I could not refuse the will of my Lord, and for the first time I was unsure of the intentions of my Lord. Was I being sent away for my safety? Or just to be kept from Aye?

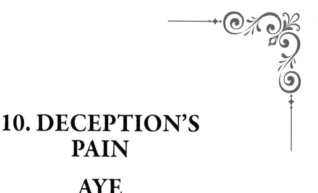

10. DECEPTION'S PAIN

AYE

So, it was once again like old times, me by my father's side until a replacement guardian was found for me. Problem was, Father did not trust anyone. On top of it, everywhere Father and I went, others would whisper secretly to each other as we walked by. As a child this belittled me. Now, I just wanted to bash their blatant skulls in.

"Aye!" Father scolded, hearing my thoughts. We stopped as I glanced up at him, seeing him arch a brow down at me. "The council meeting hopefully will not be too long, I trust you to wait in my chambers." I glanced past him seeing we were a few feet still from the audience chambers.

"Yes, Father," I said looking back at him.

"Thank you, daughter." he said, giving my shoulder a squeeze. He then took his leave from me. I watched him as he went. I knew, though, a secret dwelt in Father. He was not telling me everything. I knew I was going to request a new guardian and release Pio but...it was all off! I wanted to know the truth damn it! I was tired of being protected like I was some little china doll! I took charge, gathering up my dress and following after him.

"I want to know the truth, Father!" I called after him. I saw Father pause and look back at me as he was just about to enter into the audience chambers.

"Aye!" I heard another voice call that stopped me cold. Turned to look to see the red- curled angel coming towards me. "Alar!" She snapped, in our native tongue grabbing my arm as she pulled me aside away from Father.

"I was not finished!" I snapped back, pulling away from her grip. She just stood there looking at me stunned. Why did that look affect me so? "I...am sorry." I said, rubbing my arm where she had gripped me tightly.

"I know you are." She said softening. Strange emotions always filled me whenever I was in her presence, and nothing had changed. I truly disliked it. The same as Father, I had always wanted her to be proud of me.

"I am not giving up, you know." I protested to her.

"You do not have to, just speak to Father personally, and calmly about
it."

"Do you know Father!" I cried.

She smiled. "I do, but I do not think your demanding of your Lord is the way to go either." She said, crossing her arms over her chest. I noticed she was wearing her council robes, and I was keeping her from the meeting.

"Again, I am sorry my lady." I said curtseying.

"Talk to Father personally." she said, putting her hand on my shoulder.

"Now go wait in Father's chambers, and behave."

I curtseyed again. "Yes, my lady."

I DID DECIDE TO TALK to Father personally, and privately on this matter, but the truth did not matter anymore. I just wanted to be more than Father's favorite choice doll. I wanted to serve like all his angels did. He was my Lord just as much as he was my Father. How was I of any use! That evening Father was sitting at his desk as usual, scrolling over parchments while the harp player strummed softly in the background. Father always liked to listen to music while he worked. I rose up nonchalantly from my earthly game of chess setting my reserve. I strode over to Father's desk, slapping my hand on his desk covering his parchments.

"I want to be sent 'down there' Father."

"What?"

"I want to go to Earth. To be of use to you!"

"What put this in your mind child?"

"Father I -"

"You are not going."

"Why can't I? I want to be of use, Father! I want to serve -"

"I do not want to discuss this. Now GO!"

"FINE!" I stomped and stormed out. Why would Father not listen? Why could I not serve my Lord?! Was I defective!? Tears started to sting my eyes. I buried them deep. I was not going to cry. I knew where to go next. I gathered my dress up and dashed off.

When I arrived at her chambers, I knocked and was surprised to find she answered.

"Father still won't listen!" I said, throwing myself into her arms near tears.

She pulled me away. "Aye...I cannot help."

No! She could not say this!

"Why? What is so wrong with wanting to serve my Lord?"

"I am sorry Aye." She stood against her door waiting for me to exit. I complied, but she was not getting off that easily. I pleaded with her every day until finally, I broke her down.

"Alright!" she sighed finally. "I will bring it up with Father and with the council, now stop this insistent begging!"

I smiled happily hugging her and she wearily smiled back at me.

The next day I remained silent in hopes that the red-curled angel would talk to Father about me serving. And if Father still refused, we would bombard him together. I played the piano for Father that day while he worked again at his desk.

"You may go out to the gardens if you'd like my child." Father said looking up from his work. I stopped my playing and looked up at him puzzled.

"Don't I need accompaniment?" I asked, eyeing him suspiciously.

"No, you may go by yourself. You are not a prisoner Aye."

I rose to my feet excitedly then paused. I ran over to Father, embracing him tightly, feeling his apprehension of letting me go. It was the gardens, why would Father ever worry?

PER USUAL, I TOOK A walk through the gardens to the waterfalls. I stopped at the pool's edge, looking down into its clear crystal water. I gathered up my dress to step into the pool when a hand covered my mouth then my face was instantly slammed against the wet stone-cold wall.

"I've missed you, little miss." I heard Michael's voice purr in my ear above the roar of the falls in the background. I realized we must be inside the hidden alcoves behind the falls. "They didn't make you forget us, did they?"

I tried to move, but Michael tightened his hold around the back of my neck keeping me in place. "P...Pio..." I murmured.

"Oh, he's not here, little miss, but I am. You enjoyed me, remember?" I felt his lips graze the back of my neck and I remembered it all. I closed my eyes tight, quelling the tears as pain and guilt flooded my soul.

"Awaken to your true nature little miss. Awaken for your true Lord." Michael breathed as he let me go and I crumpled to my hands and knees, hearing Michael chuckle. I glared back at him wanting to rip his throat out.

"Such thoughts from a healer," Michael frowned, then grinned. "It would be a pleasure to be killed by beauty, because a healer you are not, my dear." A growl rose up in me as I started to lunge for him. A jolt of pain suddenly shot through my body ending it. I knew I was going to forget all this once again. This time, I think I welcomed it.

"Milady?" I heard a voice call, but I could not answer, my body was dead. "Milady?" The voice called again, oh so much closer now. "MILADY!" I heard the messenger angel gasp in horror. "Oh, my gods! What do I do? Okay, okay calm down you have this." I felt him scrape my form up in his arms as he carried me off as fast as he could.

"Pio! Sir!!"

Pio was back?

"What the hell!" I heard him cry.

"I- I-found her unconscious, and..and like this out in the gardens. I- I came to you-"

"Why me? Why didn't you bring her to her Father first?"

"I...I knew you were her guardian once. You would know what to do best!"

"Damn it!" I heard Pio mutter under his breath, feeling him take me from the worried guard as they rushed me to Father.

"Pio?" I heard Father say with concern, rising from his desk. The guard stepped forward kneeling before his Lord.

"My Lord! I am sorry I went to find her as you requested and found her like this. I-was...I didn't know what to do! I went to Pio instead of you-"

"Never mind and go fetch Raphael quickly." Father dictated.

"Yes, my Lord!" The guard rose and rushed out.

I heard Father sigh. "I tried..." he whimpered.

"My Lord, I am here!" Raphael said. flying in. I felt myself being laid down and Raphael's healing warmth started to try and heal the brokenness that was me.

"I've readjusted her seals the best I-"

"I want her in the healing waters," Father said. "Pio...I put her in your care once again. I sent you away because my mercy was needed, and that is you. You are once again her guardian."

"Of course, my Lord." I heard Pio say.

I GASPED, JOLTING UP, awake and finding myself in a bed that was not my own. At the end of the bed was a pair of light golden eyes staring at me, eyes that belonged to a woman with long white hair that cascaded down her curled-up form. She then rose up to stand and reveal she wore a simple medium length cream colored slip dress.

"She has awoken, Uriel." the woman purred. I looked past her to see Uriel step inside the room dressed in his usual robes. He smiled softly upon seeing me as I looked around me uneasily, seeing the room I was in was much smaller compared to my own chambers. The walls were undecorated and colored a sickly pale yellow and a dark wooden nightstand stood next to the bed as a form of the only furniture in the room besides the bed.

"Sorry the room is not extravagant." he began as the woman stepped off the bed to stand beside him. "But, I'm glad to see you're awake. If you like you can freshen up in the bathing pool, and then we can talk. Kyerie will show you where it is." Uriel said motioning to the woman beside him. The woman had been staring at me the whole time then she smiled, glancing back up at him. He gave a slight nod then left, leaving us alone.

"Come. I will show you where you can bathe." she said as she turned, waving the door open. I was confused but I obeyed, gathering myself out of the bed to follow after her. We entered into a large, crumbling hallway on the other side. Standing tall stood the pillars of the building as its roof, which had disappeared entirely, revealed the dark sky above. Only the checkered black and white floor remained pristine and intact with its shiny rich lacquer. There was a sense that this was once perhaps a palace. What had happened here? We came to the end of the hall as Kyerie waved her hand to reveal an opening. She motioned for me to enter and she stepped to the side. "You may bathe in here," she said. "I will bring you fresh clothes to change into."

"Thank you." I said, giving a curtsey. With an amused smile, she turned back the way we came. Well, she was charming. I thought as

I entered the bathing room to find it in no better condition. A large crack pattern could be seen in one of the stone walls, and there were chunks of stone scattered about as evidence that something once stood there. I then walked toward the bathing pool that decorated the center of the room. I slipped off my slip gown I was wearing when I paused. I smelled him! I glanced back toward the entrance, which was now sealed, but it did not matter. I knew Uriel was on the other side. I felt the sinuous hunger rise up inside me. I closed my eyes, turning back and sinking to my knees, trying to quell this savage feeling inside me.

"Here are your clothes."

I jumped, opening my eyes. "Thank you." I said quickly glancing over my shoulder to see Kyerie there again just looking at me. "Um...thank you," I repeated and saw her snap out of her entrancement. She smiled faintly then turned and left. I rose to my feet, deciding my bathing was over, and walked over to where Kyerie had set my clothes. I saw she had left a medium-length white halter dress stretched out delicately on a stone slab. I put it on to find it fit me adequately.

"You look lovely." I looked up surprised to see Uriel standing where the entrance had reappeared.

"Thank you, Uriel."

"How are you feeling?" He asked, crossing over to me.

"I-"

"Ahem."

I looked over to see Kyerie back, standing by the entrance. She was now dressed in a dark blue vest that fanned out over her shapely hip that was adorned in a short-pleated skirt. Black and white striped knee-high socks covered her legs giving her a mischievous goth appearance.

"Oh, yes you two have not been formally introduced. This is Kyerie." Uriel said, motioning to her as she smiled and crossed over to stand beside him.

"The dress looks nice on you." she said, eyeing me up and down approvingly.

"Kyerie," Uriel said sternly. She just smiled again and winked. I stared back at her in an awe of confusion.

"Excuse Kyerie," Uriel said, taking my hand and attention back. "Walk with me, will you?" I nodded as he gave a faint smile and wrapped my arm around his. We walked back out into the deteriorated halls.

"Is this wise, Uriel." Kyerie called after us. Gods this woman was driving me insane! "Her seals are broken. She is playing innocent." I froze. Damn! I glanced back up at Uriel to see him silent, his eyes closed. Looking at him, I never realized how truly beautiful Uriel was. I absently reached up to touch him when his eyes flashed open and his hand grabbed my wrist. His light autumn brown eyes now dark and stormy.

"Is this true, Aye?"

"Uriel-"

"No," he whispered, letting me go. "I love you Aye, but I will not let your seduction win." He took my hand cupping it to his cheek as I saw the pain and anguish in his eyes. *Br-ga-da.* he whispered and everything went black.

"SHE LOOKS SO INNOCENT, Uriel." Who was that? Was that Kyerie's voice?

"Well, what a better weapon than death disguised in innocence and beauty."

"At least her victims would die with a smile on their face." she smirked.

"She is more complex than a mere temptress." I heard Uriel snap.

"Testy there. You said you would not let her, but I do believe you're smitten." she teased.

"We all care for her very much. Just like even you have begun to."

"Hush." Her voice confessed. "So, what was father's fate for her? Must be big if I was called here."

"We just did not know if she would be our Aye when she awoke. I didn't know though-"

"-That this place was in shambles? How could you? You never called."

"Please, Kyerie. You know my duty is to-"

"Do as you're ordered, Uriel," she said curtly. I then felt a soft hand take mine. "We are friends, Aye. I see in time, we will meet again."

11. REUNITED

I felt a light brush against my cheek finding myself able to open my eyes to see Pio.

"Hey there," he smiled down at me. "How are you feeling?"

I paused, thinking. Why did that sound familiar? I saw Pio's smile fade as he changed the subject. "Your Father requested your presence if you feel up to it."

I nodded as I started to sit up, noticing I was in my chambers. How did I come be in my chambers? Hadn't I been somewhere before? "Come, your bath is waiting." Pio said, taking me away from my thoughts. I looked at him, seeing him offering his hand. I gave a small smile and took it as he led me to my bathing room where a bath was ready and waiting for me. "I'll fetch some sheets." I heard Pio say as I stood there just staring into the bathing pool waters watching the warm vapors rise up off the surface. The waters looked warm and welcoming. I heard Pio's return when I felt him brush my hair aside as his fingers moved to untie the short halter slip dress I was wearing, letting it fall to my feet. I looked back to him as our lips found each other in a torrid kiss. Pio, he was the one thing I knew for certain. I had missed him so much, but when did he ever leave me?

WE PROCEEDED TO FATHER'S throne room after where it was explained that Pio was to be my companion when Father could not be.

"Pio is to be your guardian and your companion for the times I cannot be. I would like to reinstate our times together, and you are to sleep in your own chambers, is that clear?"

"Yes, my Lord." I said curtseying.

That night I disobeyed my Lord sneaking to Pio 's chambers. Not wise of me, I know. I knocked on his door and he opened it, just holding a sheet around his waist. His skin and hair still damp from his bathing, gods his beauty was breathtaking to me.

"What are you doing here?" he scowled at me.

I coyly tugged at the hem of my slip dress looking down like a shy little toddler.

"I... um..."

"You shouldn't be here," he said. "Come on in."

I looked up surprised, seeing him retreat back inside as he grabbed a robe, slipping it on. I stepped inside as he came back, closing the door behind me. I looked shamefully at the floor.

"What am I going to do with you?" He said lifting up my chin to look at him then stroked my cheek with the back of his fingers. I closed my eyes, savoring his touch. I felt such love, pain, and sadness emanate from him. Why did he hurt so much? I opened my eyes looking at him wanting to take it all away.

"Yes," he said, stepping closer. "Take my pain away," he whispered, claiming my lips. Father, I am so sorry.

I JOLTED AWAKE. SHIT! I had fallen asleep in Pio's chambers! Wait where was Pio? I quickly got up, dressed then tore open his chamber door to see both Pio and Father standing there as they looked back at me.

"Aye," Father's voice boomed. "If you cannot sleep next time, come to me. Do not disturb Pio; you're only his concern when I cannot be. Is this clear?"

Is that what Pio said to his Lord? For me? For us?

"Yes, Father." I bowed.

IT SEEMED FATHER COULD not concern himself with me a lot for I was finding Pio to be my companion quite frequently. Tonight, though I was to dine with Father for certain, until I walked into Father chambers.

"Father I'm-" I paused, walking in to see Pio standing there at the dining table dressed in his regal glory. He bowed cordially. "My Lady, your father could not dine with you tonight. I hope my presence suits you just as well." I could not help but smile as he gave a little smile back. We dined together in silence with Father's guards posted by the entrance which made me feel a bit like we were being spied upon. I looked over at Pio to see him looking out the balcony doors deep in thought, well that was until I tossed a berry at him. I quickly looked back down again putting another berry in my mouth like nothing happened. I then peeked back up at him to see he was gone from his seat. I straightened up in shock as I felt a berry plop down the front of my dress.

"My, how clumsy of me let me get that for you.," I heard Pio coo behind me.

"Pio no!" I cried as I stood up from my seat. I glanced over at the guards who were still standing there straightlaced.

"I was just being gentlemanly." Pio said as I turned to face him, narrowing my eyes at him.

"Riiiight."

Pio chuckled as I reached inside my dress, pulling the berry out and threw it at him. Amazingly, he caught it. "Lucky berry," he said, holding it up. He smelled the berry.

"Mmm raspberry with essence of Aye," he popped the berry in his mouth.

"You're impossible, you know that?"

"Yep," he smiled, knocking the chair over that was between us as he pulled me boldly against him.

"AHEM." Father's voice boomed. We looked over to see Father had walked in.

"With Pio as your escort you may attend the festivities, now go before I get better judgment."

My mouth dropped. Did Father really mean this? I saw Father nod with a faint smile. I gathered my dress up and ran to Father embracing him. I then dashed to my chambers. What would I wear! A Heaven's ball was being held tonight. I was really not sure the reason for it, there was always some sort of celebration going on in Heaven. I was never allowed to attend any of them of course. I entered my chambers, surprised to see a dress had already been chosen for me to wear along with a velvet black cloak beside it. I smiled running my fingers down the plush fabric of the velvet cloak then to the dress that was a strapless white corseted bodice gown with a cascading skirt of petal ruffles. I started to dress when I heard Pio enter. I looked back behind me to see him smile as he crossed over to me, helping me out of my old dress and into my new dress lacing up the back for me. Once done, I felt his approval as he stepped back looking at me like I was the most beautiful creature to him. I smiled and he chuckled, going over to my bed and picking up the velvet cloak. He moved toward me, draping it over my shoulders and clasping the silver broach; it had to fasten together. He then raised the cowl up over my head which hung in my eyes, leaving it hard for me to see.

"I can't see."

"Stay close to me then," he said. I felt him press me tight against him and we headed off to the ball. Did Father not want anyone to know he let me attend the ball? The whole journey there I was blind until I noticed we stopped. I felt the hood release slowly off me to reveal the grand white ballroom. White carved stone pillars stood in each corner rising up to the heavenly stars that coated us like a ceiling. An angelic orchestra played by the open balcony doors while angels danced in the center of the room. Others sat in the room's decorative chaise lounges and chairs talking intently to each other, drinks in hand. The sight was truly breathtaking to me. I felt Pio unclasp the broach at my throat and remove my cloak from my shoulders. His hands then slipped around my waist from behind, pressing my back against him. I smiled, touching his hand as he drew my hand up to his lips to kiss. I turned around to face him teasingly caressing one finger down his lips, which he caught between them. I closed my eyes feeling his desire for me encase me so deliciously. A part of me wanted him to lose his noble restraints and take me right here and now, others be damned. I heard him chuckled, as I opened my eyes.

"Really now? Others be damned huh?" He kissed my hand again as his brow furrowed.

"Pio?"

"Excuse me for a moment," he said, letting my hand go.

"Why?"

"Father...he said something urgent. I am sure it is fine."

"You owe me a dance then."

"Uh...dancing is not my thing."

"Pio," I pouted.

"Okay," he smiled, caressing my cheek lightly. "I promise I owe you a dance."

He leaned in, kissing my lips lightly as he then took his leave. I turned back to the festivities before me as the orchestra's song came to an end and the dancers on the floor bowed to their partners. I smiled to myself at the beauty of all this. The orchestra then began to play another piece.

"May I have this dance?" I was surprised to see a man was standing before me. He was dressed formally in a jade-colored suit, a little out of place compared to everyone else dressed in white. His brown hair was groomed short and he wore a peacock feathered mask that covered his face. He bowed cordially, offering his hand. He then looked up and smiled charmingly, taking my hand and leading me out onto the ballroom floor. He bowed as the rest of the dancers followed suit. I looked around me uneasily, but then curtseyed following along the simple dance of the minuet. Our hands touched as we began, making me wonder who this bold man was? Others wondered also as I felt their haughty glares upon us wondering who this blasphemous man in jade was dancing with Father's blasphemous daughter. My thoughts were suddenly shattered as I sensed Pio's heated glare on my back. I tried to pull away when the jade dressed man pulled me back against him.

"You're not like the rest of them, are you?" He whispered in my ear. He then twirled me around pulling me tight back against him. "Mmm, no you are not," he cooed nuzzling against my neck breathing in the scent of me. "So sweet..." he continued as I felt the room start to swoon.

"Aye!" Pio called out.

Everything was swirling as I felt the man's hold slip from me. Then felt Pio pressed me against him his warm scent encasing me as he scooped me up in his arms, carrying me out of the ballroom. Once in the halls, he set me down, taking my face in his hands. I looked into his dark blue eyes feeling everything from him. His fear, his passion, his love, so frightfully so. I saw his biggest fear was the thought of losing me. My heart ached that he loved me so much. Yet, I did not understand why he did. His lips then claimed mine as we stumbled back against the wall. We didn't care anymore. We just wanted us. What I did not know was that this was to be our last time together.

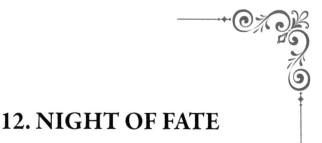

12. NIGHT OF FATE

The morning birds chirped as I awoke the next day in Pio's chambers to find Pio dressed in one of his robes, looking down at me so lovingly.

"Sleep well?"

"Yes..." I said a bit hesitantly. "Enjoy watching me sleep?"

He smiled. "In fact, I did," he said as he rose up off the bed and crossed over onto his veranda. I felt my heart sink.

"Pio?" I asked worriedly while sitting up.

"I have to go on a small mission," he said, glancing back at me. "I will be away for a while, but not too long, I'm sure."

I didn't have time to register this in my mind when a knock came at the door.

"It's a guard to take you back to your chambers. Please behave, and let the guard escort you."

I wanted to protest. I wanted to scream. This was not right! I knew why! It was due to what appened at the ball. Of course Father knew what happened. Pio had closed their connection just wanting to be with me. I obeyed, though, grabbing my dress, not even bothering to put it on. I opened the door to see one of Father's guards standing there. I looked back to Pio. He nodded as the guard escorted me away.

I SLEPT THAT NIGHT in my chambers in an uneasy rest. I suddenly awoke sensing someone was in my chambers. I carefully peeked up to see a familiar figure about to leave.

"Milady?" I said, sitting up. She turned around, and there she was, the red-curled angel. That overwhelming wave of emotions hit me again. What was this emotion whenever we were near?

"What am I to you?" I asked bluntly. She closed the door and walked over to sit beside me on the bed.

"I'm someone that cares about you very much," she said as she stroked my hair. When she rose to exit, I realized this was to be our final farewell. I knew where she was going, too; she was going "down there."

"I want to go with you!" I called out after her. She stopped, looking back at me. "You are going to 'Earth' aren't you?"

"It's not what you think, now go back to sleep."

"Yes, it is!" I said getting out of bed and crossing over to her.

She then sighed, closing the door again and she turned to face me completely.

"Fine then, my dear one, you get your wish."

THE NEXT DAY, I WAS to meet the red-curled angel in the morning at Gabriel's office. My wish was to be granted; I was going to go "down there." This was perfect! I knew Pio's missions were Earth related. I would find Pio and tell him we should stay on Earth together. Father could not forbid us then! If we could not have heaven, then we would have Earth. I arrived at Gabriel's office and knocked on the door. It opened to reveal the red-curled angel. I was relieved to see her first as she then stepped aside to reveal the intimidating Gabriel inside, sitting at his desk. He rose and I stepped inside as the red-curled angel closed the door, sealing us inside. He then picked up the quill pen from his desk offering it to me. I knew what I was doing, but why did it feel like I was sealing my fate to hell?

13. INCARNATION

Incarnation: noun in·car·na·tion \ˌin-(ˌ)kär-ˈnā-shən\ The embodiment of a deity or spirit in some earthly form.

I wore a flowing slender gown of white as I walked down the halls to the incarnation chambers with Father and Gabriel in tow. Their moods felt more like this was an execution than an incarnation. We approached the extremely tall hooded incarnation guards that stood outside the room. They wore long flowing crimson red robes that had a brocade of green gems across the front that were set in gold. I was not even sure they were angelic. Rumors said they were another creation entirely by one of Father's many siblings. Something tragic had happened to them, and Father had welcomed them here as refugees. Father spoke something to them in a language I did not understand. I saw one nod as it moved aside, opening the door for us, catching a glimpse of its long, slender fingers. We walked inside the room of circular shape as wall candles illuminated the room giving it a tranquil lit tone. In the center of the room rested a large stone slab, which I was to lay upon. I moved. laying myself down upon the stone slab.

"Begin." Father said. I gasped when a jolt hit my body, enveloping me in whiteness. The room I was in totally gone, only memories creeping up in my mind then slipping away.

"AYE! AYE! Come back!"

Aye? Was that me? Who was calling me?

"Aye I'm here we can be together!"

Pio? Who was Pio? I closed my eyes...it was too late.

PIO

What the hell was Father thinking! I looked to Father to see him look at me solemnly. The guards that held me let me go. I walked up to Father, kneeling before him.

"My Lord, I wish to resign from my status."

"Pio?"

"I wish to be assigned Earth guardian status."

I looked up seeing Father's eyes soften as he understood my intentions and nodded.

"Please watch over her Pio, protect her and don't let anything taint her."

I rose. "As you wish, my Lord." I turned to exit then paused, glancing back at Father.

"Father, why?"

"Her Mother approved, and Aye was determined. You know how Aye is."

"Yes, I do, and I know you, too, my Lord. It worked out conveniently didn't it?"

"Pio-"

I turned away from him and walked out.

I WAS NOW TO BE AN Earth guardian, or Guardian Angel as you call them. Kind of a step down on the angelic hierarchy ladder, but I did not mind. I was assigned to a newly born human female, whose soul inside resided our Aye. Incarnated, Aye had no memory of who she once was. For all stakes and purposes, she was human in every sense of the word. Born, she was raised into a family that loved her not unlike her heavenly family, and they worshiped Father devotedly. I was told Aye's human mother knew how special her new born babe would be and she, too, had promised to Father she would raise her and protect her until the time of Aye's awakening when Father called her to her mission. Things never go that smoothly though.

I WATCHED OVER AYE as she grew and matured into a beautiful, young woman. She still had those dark wavy locks that now fell just to her shoulders. Her skin was a light olive beige that blended well with her dark-caramel brown eyes, and when the light hit them just right, they illuminated an ethereal reddish-brown glow hinting to her former self that nobody knew of. I did not have time to sit and admire her much as Earth is outside of Father's haven, and our angelic souls are quite an attractive draw to the earthly, and unearthly, spirits that roamed down here just beyond the veil. Protecting her soul was of the utmost importance. For what is more tempting to the wicked than to have an amnesiac angel with untapped powers at your disposal? The war of Revelations was forever brewing. Still, it was so strange to know my Aye was inside this human form. Little things she did, though, constantly reassured me that it was indeed Aye's soul sleeping inside this human female frame. She still loved putting flowers and hair combs in her hair just as she had in what seemed like so long ago. Eventually, Aye started to wake-up. In her awakening, however, Aye awoke someone else: someone who had been waiting for so long.

14. DARK REMEMBRANCE

I thought he was perhaps a Fallen who was intrigued by her soul like so many ethereal creatures were. I watched as he would watch her from afar standing outside her bedroom window staring, hauntingly with his ethereal reddish-brown eyes. "I've found you. I've finally found you. Blood of my blood " he whispered. Troubled by this, I returned home, requesting through my commanding officer to have an audience with Father immediately.

"I need to see our Lord. "I said, bursting into his office. He looked up at me from his desk, his dark hair slicked back from his face, giving prominence to his ice blue eyes.

"Knock much," he grumbled. "And permission granted. Our Lord is expecting you. Dress appropriately."

"Right." I smirked. I entered Father's throne room still dressed in my earthly garb. I never wore those horrible robes; I was not starting now. I knelt before Father, bowing my head.

"Do I interfere, my Lord?" I asked.

Father sighed. "We knew this was inevitable, for she is outside Heaven's gates now."

"It's him, isn't it." I said looking up at Father.

"And he is out to reclaim what he thinks is his."

"Aye was never his!"

"Calm, my son. Aye belongs with us. He is stuck behind the veil. Only in dreams can he reach her. Dream walk, Pio. While the rule is you cannot show yourself physically to her, there is nothing about revealing yourself to her in dreams. Protect her. Let her know she has a choice. She does not have to become what destiny claims."

"Yes, my Lord."

The next night I stood at Aye's bedside, watching her sleep. She moaned, tossing a bit. "What are you dreaming about, Aye?" whispered.

"Well, you will soon find out." I smiled to myself as I looked behind me to see a familiar face. "Uriel."

"So, where do you want to rest?" He asked. I took a seat on the floor by the foot of Aye's bed. It seemed logical. I closed my eyes.

"Let's begin then." Uriel said as I felt him touch my forehead. "Torsvl pa- gee." he whispered.

I felt a chill shoot through me and travel down my body I gasped, opening my eyes to find myself among what looked like some 18th century ball. I looked down at myself, finding I was dressed the part too, from the white ruffled shirt, blue and gold embroidered vest under the matching waist-coat and knickers. I scanned the minds around me trying to gather information about my surroundings.

"Champaign Sir?"

The connection is shattered as I look to see a server standing before me hosting a tray of drinks. I smiled, jovially while taking a glass. "Thank you and where is our guests of honor?" I asked, looking around.

"Over there, Sir. Aciem and Achiel," he nodded. "A beautiful couple are they not?"

I look over across the room to see Aye. She was dressed in a dark maroon colored dress of the era. She stood beside who I took as Aciem. He was dressed matching in color with her, his white hair standing out in contrast as he introduced her, his bride-to-be. He gave Aye a squeeze. "Be happy, my love, this party is for you." I heard him whisper to her. He smiled as another guest came up to congratulate them shaking his hand. I saw another server come up behind him whispering something in his ear and his smile faded.

"If you will please excuse me," he said, giving a half smile to his gathered guests. He took Aye's hand and led her to the side. He caressed her cheek. "I will return. Enjoy the party." He kissed her lips lightly and he took his leave. I watched Aye as she watched him go then glanced around uneasily. She then started to move. I put my glass back on the server's tray, quickly giving pursuit as I waded through the crowd, following her out into the gardens.

"Beautiful night, isn't it?" I said, stepping up to join her. She turned to look back at me, taking me completely by surprise in her beauty. The color of her dress against her long dark locks and cream skin complimented her very well. "...And congratulations by the way."

She furrowed her brow at me turning to look back out at the gardens.

"You do not seem so happy about it. Maybe he is not the one you love." She spun to face me as I smiled, taking her hand bringing it to my lips, lightly kissing it. She looked up at me amazed by my words then pulled her hand away. "You've asked yourself that, haven't you?" She looked away solemnly as I turned her face to look back at me. I stepped in closer and claimed her lips. I pulled away, my eyes still closed to hear the sweetest word ever whispered.

"Pio?" I opened my eyes to see her looking up at me with tears sparkling to the brink. "It's you." she said, reaching up to caress my face. I held her hand there savoring her touch.

"Yes, my love, it's me." I smiled. She remembered me, she remembered us! The joy was short-lived, though, as I felt my presence had been discovered.

"Pio?" Aye asked worriedly, sensing my distress.

"It seems the spell has been broken my dear." We both looked back inside, hearing disturbances from within. I took Aye's face in my hands not wanting her to look. "You have to wake up now." I allowed my hands to slip from her face as I pulled out a small gold handled dagger from inside my coat pocket. She looked down at it then, back up to me.

"FIND HIM!" A voice shouted from inside. Aye nodded as I gripped her arm pulling her against me, impaling the blade into her.

"I love you." I whispered. Her body started to slip limp in my arms as I lowered her to the ground gently.

"THERE HE IS!" A voice cried out. I then took the dagger, plunging it into myself.

"NO!" A voice screamed.

I smiled, as death met me in blackness. I suddenly jerked awake to find myself back in Aye's room. I jolted up to check on Aye to see her sleeping peacefully and breathing. This scenario went on night after night. Her brother would seduce her away in a different dream, a different setting. I would seduce her back. Only to have her forget everything upon waking, or so I thought. Father finally intervened in our little game, managing to block Aye from her brother's senses, which I am sure made him totally pissed. Still, I could not keep away. Father didn't say I could not go back into her dreams. I got comfy once again and closed my eyes letting my mind drift. When I opened them again, I found myself standing in an empty hallway. Brown colored lockers lined the walls on each side along the checkered brown floor. I spotted Aye further down the hall closing her locker door. I smiled to myself, ah dreaming of high school how cute. She looked sweetly sexy in her school uniform of a pleated dark navy-blue skirt with a white button-down shirt, which she wore stylishly untucked. She then sensed my presence glancing over at me. I gave her a slight smile and started to walk over.

"Who are you?" she asked as I reached her.

"I do wish you'd remember," I said, leaning back against a locker, "but I am not the bad guy."

"No...you are not... " she said, observing me as though trying to remember. I smiled at her words.

"*Piorrr*" A voice growled. I frowned as I looked over to see a tall, horned-helmet samurai demon standing there. Its white frizzled hair peeked out from under its helmet along with a deteriorating face and glowing yellow eyes.

"So, you know my name. I must be famous."

It drew its sword. "Puny angel" it growled.

"Yeah, that's what they all say." I rubbed my hands together crouching down, placing my palm on the ground. "Mi-ca-loz!" Lightning rose up from underneath the creature, engulfing it as it screamed and convulsed into dust. Its armor clanked to the floor. I rose up and looked back at Aye. "Your dreams are awesome, but let's change this scenery, shall we?" I snapped my fingers and we were standing on top of a medieval tower overlooking the forested land below. Aye looked around in amazement. "You can control your dreams, you know."

She looked back at me. "Are you my guardian angel or something?" she asked sarcastically. What the hell? I thought. I confessed. "Indeed, I am," I answered as I crossed over to her, taking her hand to shake. "I'm Pio, nice to meet you." I smiled.

She smiled coyly. "Um...about controlling your dreams?"

"To do so is within you, as are a lot of things, aren't there?"

"And to voice them would land me in a nice padded cell. Which sounds nice at times."

"Voices that make you think Father spoke to you? Feeling you don't belong, memories, feelings, an ache you can't explain."

"Yeah," she said, bowing her head.

"You can talk to me, if you like. We can meet like this every night. You know my name now. Just invoke my name and I will be here waiting." She looked back up at me, narrowing her gaze. No more secrets, I thought. "You know, he's not the one that loves you." I paused. "...It's me." I leaned in, wondering if she would pull away, but she did not as my lips met hers. Then, like in a fairy tale, the spell was broken and we were reunited once more. The only problem was, I was an angel and she was now human. Talk about your long-distance relationships.

15. BECOMING HUMAN

At that point, I swore then and there to become human for Aye. I once again requested an audience with Father. I wondered how he would take this. When my audience was granted with Father, I knelt down on one knee before his throne, bowing my head.

"Father, I request to become human for Aye...I want to be with her."

Father let out a sigh. "I will grant your request Pio, but only when the time is right and it can be safely done. I have told Aye this as well."

"Aye came to you for me?" I said looking up at him surprised. Father then rose up off his throne.

"Yes, you were always in her prayers." I rose as well.

"Thank you, Father." I bowed. All should have been fine, but Heaven's time and Earth's time were quite different. Patience also was never a virtue with Aye. Aye overcame herself with worry as to when the right time would be. Father would not lie to us, would he? It was nice to see her ability to emotionally overload was still intact. I tried to sooth her the best I could, but I had to admit I started to wonder myself. What did Father mean till the time was right? Only in dreams did we have each other. I then made a terrible mistake that nearly lost me Aye forever. I did what we angels call "ghosting." Basically, it is possession but, hey, we're the good guys. It was also strictly taboo. The humans are left unharmed often thinking like they were under some magic spell, or had too much to drink, you get the idea. I went to my friend Razz to learn this craft. I wanted to physically be with Aye, even if it was just for a moment. I knew Razz knew how to do this, but the question was would he show me this taboo? I knocked on his chambers and it opened, revealing Razz.

"I never thought you'd be a rebel Pio." He said, closing the door behind me as I walked in.

"You got my message and know then?"

"I did. I just never thought."

"Well, I never thought your gorgeousness could look like hell so we are even."

Razz smiled and laughed. "Hey this is how a rebel looks, my friend, get used to it." I gave a slight smile back, but did wonder what my friend had gotten himself into. He did look so worn and tired. I knew, though, he had his own path to go down, and so did I.

Once I learned the craft, the next step was to find a suitable human male body to possess. I told myself this would just be for a brief time, no harm done. I just wanted to truly be with Aye. To touch her, smell her. Gods to taste her again! Then the unthinkable happened, Aye conceived while I was in this human shell. The Heavens came thundering down. I was instantly relieved of my Earth Guardian status, and brought before my commanding officer by two guards. "You know I've been waiting for you to screw up," he chided. "I've heard about you being Father's little favorite."

"Well, it seems you're going to have to wait longer, he's mine." A familiar voice quipped.

My commanding officer's smile faded as he looked past me. "Raphael?" I looked back behind me to confirm it was indeed Raphael. "How so?" My commanding officer said.

"Because... I said so." Raphael smiled. A blinding flash filled the room. Once it was over, I found myself in an all too familiar room. I turned around to see Father standing out on his balcony.

"Father, I want to see Aye!"

"Pio you can't see her. She's banished you from her." he said with a painful tone in his voice. "As a human she has the power to do so. Even if you tried, she would not remember you."

"Why?"

"I put her back to sleep. Nothing of angels or demons will haunt her mind during this time. It's only temporary, do not worry."

"The child..."

"The child is what it is. Aye's soul is in a human body. It's what I created them to do: breed!"

"You know I will still watch over her."

"As I am expecting you to." Father said.

Ignorance was bliss once more for Aye and the unborn child that grew inside her. The child that I could not help but wonder was in part mine?

"Don't do that you'll give yourself a headache."

I smiled looking back behind me to see Father. "I guess I've been on earth too long. The whole science and spiritual thing can get confusing."

"Watching Aye from afar I see." Father said, nodding to my standing by his looking glass. I wave away the scene of Aye sleeping away as I turn to face him.

"I am sorry. I hope you don't mind."

"I don't, and his name is Zadkiel."

"What?"

"The child. You've reached out to the child, right? You felt it."

"I wasn't..."

"You see, it is written. Zadkiel is said to be the angel of mercy and forgiveness. You Pio are the manifestation of my mercy. Zadkiel is the angel of mercy. Zadkiel is on my list but I have no recollection of making an angel of mercy other than you. So, it seems he is yours." Father smiled as he crossed over, waving his hand over his looking glass to bring back the scene of Aye sleeping. "And in due time Aye will remember... she will remember everything."

SO, NOW IT WAS TIME for Aye to awaken again and this time, she was to know her whole truth. Along with this I had promised to become human for Aye once again. I would do it right this time and we would be together. Father kindly agreed as well as preparing the soul transfer process. We use this technique when we need to harbor an "at ready use" human body for earthly missions. Unlike possession, where the human soul is still intact, a soul transfer is where the human soul is on the brink of exiting the body and we then take possession of it. A soul transfer carries the same risk as an incarnation in which the angel may lose all memory of itself, so as to only cling to the thoughts and memories of the previous host. It was a risk we both understood. Aye's and my connection would also be down during this time, so we both needed to be prepared. Aye was unsure she could handle not feeling my presence, but soon, I would be human for her. I would be able to touch her, hold her. That was all that mattered.

IT WAS SOON JUDGMENT day as a willing vessel had been found. I was halfway through the transition process when it felt like every particle in my being had exploded and my soul was thrashed back home. What the hell had happened?

"Send me back!" I growled, trying to pull my naked form up from the stone floor.

"Your woman has betrayed the Heavens," a voice scowled.

"Betrayed the Heavens!" Another voice hissed, echoing after it. What has my precious Aye done now? I then passed out. When I came to, I found myself in the healing waters. Suddenly, the gurgling sound of water draining began, as I felt the water retreat around me and the pod door opened.

"Welcome back," Raphael said, hovering over me.

I tried to talk, wanting to say Aye, only to find guttering sounds coming out.

"You have a one-track mind don't you, boy." Raphael said. "Well, it seems you have a rival." he said, troubled.

"Wh-hat?" I managed to spit out starting to rise as searing pain screamed through my body then out of me.

"Relax, Pio," Raphael soothed, laying me back down. "We will get Aye back, but your soul has to finish healing. You were nearly torn apart. You're going to need intense therapy to get your mobility back."

"F...Fine then we start tomorrow," I said, gritting through my teeth.

"Seriously, Pio-"

"Tomorrow. With or without you."

"The healer gets no respect, does he?"

I tried to give my best smile. Gods, it even hurt to smile. "Apparently not."

"Tomorrow then," Raphael concluded.

The next day the training grounds were ours.

"I'm a healer, not a warrior mind you, so be gentle with me." He smirked, picking up a sword and twirling it in his hand.

I chuckled as I crossed over to pick up my sword. "I will," I smirked back when suddenly everything went black.

"PIO! PIO! CAN YOU HEAR ME!" I heard him, but I just could not respond. "HEALING WATERS NOW AND NOTIFY OUR LORD!"

I wondered if this was how Angels die.

WHEN I HAD FULLY RECOVERED, I decided to pay a visit to this rival. The window on the upper floor of his modern home estate was open, with light illuminating from inside so I took this as an invitation. I flashed inside.

"I thought you'd show." I heard a voice say as I looked around the modern renaissance styled bedroom to find my rival standing there in the entrance way. He was about an inch shorter than me and his brown hair was groomed short in modern male style. He wore a navy-blue button-down shirt with white buttons and black slacks. The coloring brought out his eerie light green eyes; he was a Nephilim.

"Then you must know you have something of mine," I finally spoke.

"She belongs to you?" He questioned, leaning against the door frame and crossing his arms over his chest. "She belongs with us. We're more kindred to her than you are."

"Aye is neither fallen nor Nephilim."

He smiled. "She's no angel either."

"True," I said, crossing over to the fireplace that was against the far wall and something on the mantle caught my eye. It was a small silver music box with gold etching around it with a golden peacock on the lid. "Is she here?" I said, picking up the music box feeling his intense glare on me.

"What if she is? Your Lord has locked her soul out from Heaven because she refused to part from her new family."

"Really?" I said intrigued, looking back over to him. "I must have been out of commission longer than I thought." I placed the music box back down, turning my full attention back to him.

"How did you convince her, if you don't mind my asking?"

"You were an illusion. I was real. I was now. I was flesh. Sure, your soul transfer could have worked, but you would wake up not knowing who you were. Once you did remember, you then have to find her. Come on, do you think your father was going to make it easy for you two?"

"For a Nephilim you sure know a hell of a-" Then it hit me, the Heavens ball!

The Nephilim smiled again at my realization. "Yes, yes, that was me, and my sister too. She does a mean Yahweh impersonation doesn't she?"

"How the hell-"

"I was hired by her brother," he said annoyingly, crossing over to sit on the edge of the room's large bed "...only I kind of turned the tables on him. Aye's a keeper, isn't she?" He grinned.

In a way I was thankful, but not so much.

"We shall see." I said then flashed out. Returning home, I found out sadly he was right about everything. In anger, Father had indeed banished Aye's soul from home due to her refusal to see him. Her connection to us was blocked. In part, she was now a Fallen. So, what did I do next? I just stole her soul and sent it to purgatory. Was Aye dead? No, but a strange deadly illness befell the human land and of course Aye is human. Aye would seek redemption whether she liked it or not. I knew she still loved me. I tried to make her stew in her cell for a bit, but all too soon I found myself outside her cell door. Against the grey stone wall, she was dressed in a long flowing-sleeved empress-styled gown; her head was bowed as her arms were arched out, her wrists shackled to the wall. I decided to make my appearance, nodding to the short hooded guard to unlock her door. He went over and pulled out his keys, unlocking the door. I gave him a thankful touch on the arm as he stepped aside, leaving. I walked inside, removing the hood of my cloak then unfastening it as I let it fall to the ground. I had worn my old uniform, from when I was her guardian back home. It felt so odd to wear it again but seemed fitting somehow. I crossed over closer to stand before her.

"You know you can ask for redemption."

She looked up at me and I saw her reddish-brown eyes were now completely red. He had awakened her dark nature. This was good, as I knew Aye had to embrace it not hide from it like Father had insisted, it must be.

"Why?" She spat. "Is it because I am free? That I know the truth now," she spurned. "I've done nothing wrong!"

I knelt down in front of her. "Because I know you still love me." I said. I started to unbutton my tunic and watched as her gaze drifted to watching me. I then reached over slicing into my flesh using the dragon claw ring I wore and closed my eyes, waiting. I heard the jingle of her chains. I remembered her kind's secret blood lust as I felt the lap of her tongue at my chest. Her lips then sealed around the wound and I gave into the pleasure, cradling her head to my chest, letting her feed until I felt she had enough.

"That's enough now love, "I said, pulling her away. I cupped her face in my hands, lifting it to look up at me. "You still love me, I know it." I said as my gaze drifted to her lips colored with my life. Before I knew what, I was doing I pressed my lips against hers, tasting our essences combined. I felt her passion stir as our kiss deepened. Yes...she still loved me.

In the end Aye's soul was redeemed and her connection to Heaven had been restored. Then I left her alone to be human. I returned to my chambers one day, which now was on the upper levels due to my soul being nearly torn apart. I paused, seeing my friend Razz's original choice for me, Ne'nel, standing by my door. My, news flies fast in heaven.

"Ne'nel, "I said, playing innocently confused.

She gave a slight smile. "I...I heard about you, and I was concerned." she said worriedly. "There were rumors you'd died."

I smiled chuckling. Got to love Heaven's rumors. "Would you like to come inside?" "I said.

She smiled, surprised. "O...kay. "

So, I let Ne'nel hover over me. She consoled me, soothed me, told me how horrid Aye was. How she was not deserving of me. I would just smile charmingly at her like she was the most mesmerizing woman to me. Which often got her to fluster and blush. And then I oddly saw Aye. You see though an angel may be earthbound, our souls can return home when we sleep, or while in deep mediation. I was walking down the halls with Ne'nel by my side when I saw her. Aye saw me too, and with Ne' nel.

"Let's go," I heard Ne'nel snap as she tugged at my arm and we continued on our way walking past. When we got to my chambers, I went over to pour myself a drink. "I saw the way you looked at her," Ne'nel said with a jealous tone to her voice. I smiled as I turned to look back at her.

"Guess I was making the wrong one jealous." I walked over to her, taking her hand, and kissed it. "I am sorry. I still love Aye." I let her hand go and went to find Aye. I arrived, knocking on her chamber's door.

"Pio?"

I turned around to see her standing there, holding some books in her arms and looking at me puzzled.

"Where is your friend," she asked a bit jealously. I tried to hide a smile as I nonchalantly stepped closer to her.

"You're jealous?"

"No," she said, glancing away. I lifted her chin up to look back at me.

"You're lying," I said as I nonchalantly walked her against the wall. I then kissed her lips and her books fell to the floor and her arms slipped around my neck. I broke away as she pressed her forehead against mine.

"You're a jerk, you know that," she pouted.

"I know. And how should I feel about you?"

"He helped me understand who I am. Plus, you could have been a figment of my imagination for all I knew."

"I was on my way Aye!"

"Like Father would plop you right next door to me!" She said, pulling back from me tiredly.

"I know." I sighed. "Doesn't mean I have to like it. You belong to me."

"Really now?" She said, arching her brow.

"Yes, really now." I said, smiling darkly as I claimed her lips faintly. My lips then trailing to her neck.

"You are my master. she breathed. I pulled away looking down at her.

"Am I now?" I smirked.

"I choose you to be," she said, draping her arms around my neck. "Only you can tame my hunger, sate it," she cooed as she teased back, kissing my lips lightly. Damn could she be seductive. It was hopeless; I could not be mad at her. I could not resist her either as I responded to her kiss. We were master and slave to each other. In the end I became Aye's guardian and lover once more. And I swore I would become human for Aye.

ANGELIC CONFESSIONS: SPECIAL EDITION

For more Angelic goodness visit

https://authorjanmarie.wix.com/
angelicconfessions

Follow Jan Marie on
Facebook @Janny-JanMarie-C
X (formerly Twitter) @AuthorJanMarie
Instagram @authorjanny_janmarie_c
And if you enjoyed this book, please be kind and leave a review.